the tomb of reeds

the tomB of reeds

Sarah Baylis

Julia MacRae Books

A DIVISION OF FRANKLIN WATTS

© 1987 Sarah Baylis
All rights reserved
First published in Great Britain
1987 by Julia MacRae Books
A division of Franklin Watts
12a Golden Square, London, W1R 4BA
and Franklin Watts Australia
14 Mars Road, Lane Cove, NSW, 2066

British Library Cataloguing in Publication Data
Baylis, Sarah
The tomb of reeds.
I. Title
823'.914[F]   PR6052.A8/
ISBN 0–86203–279–2

Designed by Douglas Martin
Typesetting by Computape (Pickering) Ltd
Printed and bound in Great Britain by
Billings of Worcester

contents

dedicated to Nicky

THE FEASTS OF THE CELTIC YEAR – There were four main feasts in the Celtic year. The year began on what is now the first of November with the Feast of *Samain*. Three months later on the first of February was *Imbolc* followed by the feast of *Beltine* or *Cétshamain* on the first of May. The fourth feast was that of *Lugnasad* on the first of August. Of these four *Samain* and *Beltine* were the more important and in the myths many important events took place on these days . . .

Larousse Encyclopaedia of Mythology

the song of amhairghin

I am the womb of the earth,
I am the stag of seven points,
I am the wide flood on the plain,
I am the wind on deep water,
I am the blaze on the hillside,
I am the shining tear of the sun,
I am the hawk on the clifftop.
I am fair among the flowers,
I am the oak and the lightning that blasts it,
I am the queen of hives,
I am the giant who wields a sharp sword,
I am the salmon in a dark pool.
I am the shield for every heart.
I am the hill of poets,
I am the ravening boar,
I am the roaring winter sea,
I am the wave that returns to the shore,
And only I know the secret of the tomb.

part one

1. BRÍOEY

I am the womb of the earth . . .

"Go on home, now. And tell mother I will be back in good time for dinner."

Bridey settled herself in the coracle and waited for the wild rocking to subside before pushing her oar against the bank and steering the little boat through the rushes towards the open water.

"Go on, now, Eadha," she called to her brother. "You can't come today, there's no time, I've too much to do." But the boy lingered on the bank, with a woeful expression on his face and his fingers twisting the frayed hem of his tunic. He was plump and dirty and his black hair had come untied. He glared through it at his older sister, and as Bridey waved from the water – a swaying circle within a ring of ripples – he stuck out his tongue sulkily.

"I don't mind about your stupid old boat," he cried, turning and stomping back up the grassy bank towards the settlement.

The girl laughed and pulled on her paddle, sending the little boat into a spin. She let herself revolve, watching the sparkling water, the distant settlement, and the tiny figure of her retreating brother pass before her eyes, once, twice . . . round and round. Soon the frantic motion made her dizzy, so dipping her paddle into the water to stop the coracle she began pulling steadily for the centre of the lake. She would not go far, for the current was strong near the middle and she could see the grey line of fast water where the river flowed southwards from its source in the mountains. This lake, a sheet of shining water, was one of many formed by the great river as it travelled across the plains to the sea. Miles of marshland, dotted with small isolated settlements, lay between here and the rocky coastline. It was a flat place, populated mainly by birds.

As soon as she was far enough from the shore to savour her freedom, she started heading for the willows that grew along the shoreline a mile from home. She was dazzled by the sun on the water, and the light made her narrow her eyes and duck her head. The air was cool but the sun felt warm on her arms and shoulders. The last of the early mist was disappearing and by noon it would be hot. Bridey tugged at the rusty pin and shrugged off her cloak. She pulled her tunic up over her bare knees and took off her shoes. The wide lake and cloudless sky filled her with happiness, and it seemed as if nothing in the world could threaten her contentment – not even the prospect of long hours toiling under a hot sun. It was good to get away from the settlement and from her family for a few hours, to hear nothing but the murmuring water and the early conversations of the birds. She was not an unsociable girl but she often longed to be solitary; at times her family drove her to distraction and she fled from them with a physical distaste, astonished that she could love them and hate them within a moment. She was fickle, churlish, ungrateful – thirteen years old. Within her an angry child and a grown woman battled furiously.

Bridey was a willow-gatherer. Ever since people had come to live on the shores of the lake her family had gathered willow wands, dried them, split them, and made the smooth wicker into any kind of basket, cradle or covering that anyone in the settlement or the neighbouring farmsteads ever needed. It was a skilled and respected craft. Bridey's mother had taught her daughters much of the sacred lore of the willow-gatherers, and on winter evenings she might recount some of the tales from the dark past when her great-grandmothers would prepare the wicker-men for the Druids of Erin. These wicker-men were huge hollow statues in human shape but with blank, blind eyes – and Bridey's mother would drop her voice to a whisper as she told of the Beltine fires kindled at the feet of these wicker giants, and of the dreadful screams of the criminals and prisoners trapped inside as the flames leaped higher and the black smoke rose into the spring twilight, coiling and wreathing in soft, sickening billows.

But those were heathen times and now the willow was used for nothing more harmful than a winnowing basket or a tray for goose eggs. Bridey's own grandmother would often remind the girl of the beneficial qualities of the holy willow: "My child, there has never been a better remedy for the rheumatics, of that I'm sure," and she would smile knowingly, whispering, "It's a tree of great enchantment, a tree of poetry. Remember, burn not the Willow, for she is sacred to poets." Then Bridey would laugh and reassure her grandmother she would do no such thing.

She paddled on, lost in thought, until she entered the willow grove and steered the coracle under the branches. She was far away, dreaming of the past and of the shadowy figures that lived there. Who had they been, her ancestors, and why so savage and wild? Had they been so unlike herself, or had they sometimes felt as she did – filled with unexpected happiness on a summer's morning? Had they really been as terrible and as awesome as they sounded?

The water was deep where the willows dug into the bank and Bridey could climb up the ancient roots as if they were a ladder. She pulled the coracle after her and turned it over in the sun to dry. A slight dampness about her knees and feet warned her that the coracle's skins needed another coating of resin to render them watertight.

She took a broad knife from her belt and began to hack long fronds from the overhanging branches – a few here, a few there, but never enough to do real damage to the trees. She climbed along the twisted branches, hanging over the water to watch the trout glide through the weeds, glimpsing her own reflection between the leaves. She enjoyed her strength and surefootedness on the creaking boughs, and the easy way she tossed the leafy wands down to the bank. Overhead was a rustling canopy, below the brown water of the lake.

After an hour she had enough for two large bundles and she sat down to strip away the silvery leaves. As she worked her mind drifted here and there, only half aware of the sun and the birdsong and the striped shadows beneath the trees. She was remembering Beltine. Not the Beltine of her ancestors, but the festival held earlier this year in Saille, the month of the Willow.

She had not been so happy then, and life had seemed hard and difficult. She hated the cold weather and this year the winds across the lake had gnawed at her bones and chapped her lips, and the marshes had been sheeted with ice month after month. It was as if spring would never come. She was always at odds with her mother and older sisters, and even Eadha had driven her mad with his clinging dependence and never-ending demands. But since then everything had changed, for her oldest sister had married and gone to the neighbouring settlement, while Sorcha, the remaining sister, was rarely home, spending most of her time visiting friends or taking baskets through the woods to sell. Bridey was glad of it: home was quieter now with only Eadha left – and he could be fun at times. At eight years old he was less and less the whining baby of the family. He was a cautious sturdy boy, and Bridey liked him more and more. He talked too much; but then, she reflected, all children chatter interminably. She relished the new peacefulness at home without her sisters, the extra attention her mother paid her – and more room in bed at night.

Beltine came while the willows were clad in their first grey leaves and the twigs hung heavy with yellow catkins. The people decked the houses with green boughs to bless the milk for the summer. They piled high the fires – two mighty pyres between which the cattle were driven, their tails high and their eyes wide with fright. The flames would keep them free of sickness and the ashes from the fires, scattered on the fields, would save the crops from blight.

Bridey had laughed and clapped her hands, she had sung and chanted and beaten on the drum, dancing in the fields by torchlight. Everything would be all right after Beltine, for winter was over and her sisters were growing up and leaving –

no more of their criticism from now on; no more bad feelings and jealousy.

Now in the middle of summer she was still feeling the benefits of this new-found freedom, though she was dismayed to find that she missed her sister more than she had expected. Her mother laughed and teased her, "It will be you going off with a lad one of these mornings," and she winked, "leaving me with only the boy to fetch my willow for me." Bridey frowned and declared that she had no intention of leaving.

After the wands were free of leaves, Bridey deftly wound a length of branch round the whole bundle and tied it securely. One of the bundles she would take back today, the other she would fetch tomorrow, for the little boat would turn belly-up if she took them both at once.

She loved her coracle and allowed no one else to use it. It was hers alone. She tended it and repaired it when it sprang a leak. She loved its frantic progress over the lake. She had waited years to get it. First it had been her father's, then after his death five winters ago it had passed to the two elder daughters. Only since Beltine had Sorcha let Bridey take it out on the lake, and now, not learning from her own experience, Bridey taunted Eadha with her new possession. Why should she share, she asked herself, if they had not? She smiled at the thought of his sulky face. Perhaps she would give him a ride tomorrow; she would not be able to bear his pleading much longer.

There was only one thing she wanted more than her little boat, only one thing she would exchange it for, and that was a horse: a tall horse with a flowing mane and rolling eyes, that would carry her over the plain, faster and faster . . . The horses in the settlement weren't worthy of the name – fat ponies that plodded on sturdy legs; no grace or nobility about them. Cron, the brown pony they used for carrying baskets to sell, would never gallop anywhere. It was hard enough to make him break into a trot.

Bridey had seen real horses long ago when a group of the King's men passed by the lake on their way to the mountains. How beautiful they were, both the horses and their riders. She still thought of the men and wondered where they were going, so proud and silent in their fur-lined cloaks. They galloped through her daydreams and she longed to be with them, riding off to war at the command of the King.

Leaning down she dropped the coracle back into the water. She splashed her hot skin with water and stooped to drink, then stepping in she carefully balanced the bundle of willow before her and turned the boat in the direction of the settlement. Keeping near the bank this time she began to paddle slowly home.

"There you are!" exclaimed her mother, coming to the door and beckoning her daughter. Bridey staggered over and threw down the bundle, wiping her face with the hem of her tunic.

"By the Saint! It's hotter here than on the water," she said and sat down panting.

"Is that all you've brought, girl?" asked her mother, looking at the pile of willow wands. "Have you forgotten the order from the convent, and the new baskets needed? We could do with new panniers for Cron and . . ."

Bridey groaned and looked up sourly.

"There's another load left by the grove," she said through clenched teeth. "I'll fetch it tomorrow when . . ."

"You'll fetch it today, child, as soon as you have eaten your food, for we need to start weaving tomorrow or we'll be too late."

"Leave me alone!" Bridey urged silently, hot and irritable. Out loud she said, "All right, all right, but there's no great hurry." Perhaps she could have a swim this afternoon and lie in the sun for an hour before going back to fetch the second bundle. She brightened at the thought. "Where's my sister?"

"Right behind you, Bridey," said Sorcha, and poked her head above a waving forest of wicker. Bridey turned and laughed at her perspiring face. Sorcha was sorting lengths of willow for weaving, "And losing patience waiting for you to come back from your dilly-dallying. There's two of the *clocháin* at the convent need mending, and all the chairs, and twenty baskets to be ready within the week . . . "

Bridey sighed more deeply. It was too hot for hard work today. Behind her she could hear her mother:

" . . . and after that you must go and see Mother Abbess and tell her the roofing will be late. She wants you to go to the woods for her. She says she has some errand for you to run up there – though who knows what she can want, and it's not as if we can spare you here."

"Yes, Mother," Bridey replied sullenly, and she picked up the bundle and carried it to the cowshed. She went into the little house for her meal, cursing her family and wishing she lived alone on the other side of the lake. Nothing had changed.

It was dark inside the hut and full of the smell of baking bread, sweet and yeasty and warm. Her mouth began to water as she crouched down opposite Eadha who was already half-way through a bowl of vegetable stew. His dark head was bent over the bowl and he seemed intent on his food, but as Bridey broke off a piece of bread he looked up and gave her a shrewd stare.

"I have a secret that I will never tell you," he declared, and he screwed up his eyes and pursed his lips before bending back over his bowl.

"Oh, what can it be, little brother?" said Bridey sardonically. "What can a little tit-bit like you have found that could possibly be of interest to me?"

"That I shall never tell," he said solemnly, his mouth full and his sticky fingers scratching his head.

Bridey shrugged.

"Don't tell then, boy," she said, though she could see he was bursting with the news, "because I don't mind a bit about your stupid old secret," and she bent her head to hide her smile.

Eadha looked perplexed. The urge to tell fought with the desire to keep silent and he was becoming pink with the effort. Then his mother and Sorcha came noisily into the hut and his agony was prolonged: if he had any news, it was for Bridey's ears alone. He hugged himself and vowed to keep silent.

2. the aBBess

I am the stag of seven points ...

The convent lay half a mile away across the fields. The quickest way to reach it was to follow the path that led through the marshes, then clamber up a wooded slope until the low wooden buildings came into sight. Around the refectory and oratory, a scattering of *clocháin* cells stood like beehives in the grassy clearing – they were in sore need of repair, not yet mended after the ravages of the long winter. Sheltering the convent from the winds that blew across the lake stood a line of ancient oak trees, where druids still gathered wood for their Midsummer fires, and in the shelter of these trees a small plot of land showed where past convent women had been laid to rest in the damp earth.

Bridey's feet were wet from crossing the marshes and she stopped to put on her shoes before striding up the slope beneath the shade of the oak trees. The sound of her footsteps in the twigs made the birds shriek in alarm and the tree-tops echoed with their cries; but soon she left the shade of the woods and was standing in the clearing on cropped turf starred with daisies and dandelions. It was silent except for a low murmuring that came from the cells where some of the women had retreated to sit in solitary contemplation and chant their endless liturgies. The sound of prayers seemed to intensify the silence rather than diminish it.

A tall column of smoke rose from the centre of the clearing where a crackling fire was being tended by one of the convent women, and as Bridey ran over she straightened up and smiled.

"Good day, Bridey, what brings you here?"

"Mother Abbess wants me," explained the girl, and stepped back as a gust of wind blew smoke in her face. Eyes smarting, she saw the woman point towards the stone building on the edge of the clearing.

"She's yonder, in the sanctuary," and she tossed more grass on the fire with her pitchfork.

Bridey thanked her and walked away. As she approached the sanctuary she passed a tall stone covered in ciphers and spiralling patterns. Carved crudely onto one side of the stone was a picture of St. Brigit, and Bridey bowed her head and murmured a prayer. It was after St. Brigit that she herself was named. She had been born at Candelmas, and Candelmas was St. Brigit's day, marking the end of winter.

The convent had always been there, a centre of learning beside the marsh. It was dedicated to the ancient goddess Brigit, though some of the women studied the new faith of the Nazarene, brought from across the sea by thin Christians. Night and day the women kept Brigit's holy fire burning. It was said by some that the cows of the convent would never run dry, and spring would reign as long the holy fire remained tended. Others even claimed to have seen Brigit's shadowy form as she passed through the woods on summer evenings, and to have heard her voice and seen the bright shamrock spring up beneath her feet. Bridey knew nothing of such matters. For her, Brigit was not just a holy saint, but also a warrior of the ancient stories, whose exploits she remembered from countless bedtime stories – Goddess of poetry, healing and smithcraft, Queen of all Erin.

She knocked on the carved door of the sanctuary, but received no answer. She pushed open the door to find the Abbess bending over a rough wooden table, consulting the oracular sticks. She had thrown them onto a white cloth and was studying them with an expression of great concentration, sucking her bottom lip and frowning, as if through willpower alone to force the sticks to render up their secrets. At her elbow, propped open with an ink-horn, was a tall book, beautifully illuminated and decorated with spirals and flourishes. Nearby a tall candle dripped wax on to the floor, filling the room with a smell of beeswax.

"Mother?"

Abbess Fionnuala looked up crossly. She had the same shrewd green eyes and determined brows as Bridey, though her hair was streaked with grey and her skin lined with age.

"Yes, what do you want, girl?" she snapped. "Can you not see that I'm busy?" Her scowl was ferocious. She was often stern, and children feared her, but they still came to her for stories.

Bridey flushed and stammered indignantly, "My m-mother sent me! I was told you needed me."

The Abbess stared at her in annoyance, but then her face relaxed and she smiled and held out her hand.

"I'm sorry, Bridey, my dear," she said. "I didn't mean to snap your head off, but these predictions are hard to fathom – and the heat puts me out of humour. Come over here and sit down, and let me try to remember why I sent for you." She rose and went to the window where a pitcher of milk stood in the shade, and pouring two bowls she handed one to Bridey – "Here, drink this and we will sit down and catch up on our news." They settled down by the table and Bridey rested her elbows on the scratched surface and looked at the white cloth.

"What have the sticks been telling you, Mother?"

The Abbess sighed.

"Very little, my dear. I think I'm losing my powers. Perhaps I have angered our dear Brigit in some way. I lack inspiration and my brain feels as thin as gruel." She shrugged and smacked her lips, "Never mind – this milk makes me feel more cheerful."

Bridey smiled. She was accustomed to Fionnuala's temper and the sharpness of her tongue, for the Abbess was not blessed with patience and had been known to break a roomful of pots at the height of her rage. But usually Bridey was at ease and only seldom – if Fionnuala was distracted or irritable – did she feel any resentment, or remember that she was a basket-weaver and not a woman of power who could read books and interpret the oracular sticks.

They sat together and talked, and Bridey told the Abbess of the likelihood of the baskets being late. "Especially if I sit here idling," she sighed, but Fionnuala patted her hand and told her to rest where she was. Bridey settled back and listened to the Abbess, laughing at her jokes and asking eagerly after the women of the convent. Half an hour had passed before they were disturbed by a shout from outside. They went to the window to see the woman who had been tending the fire running towards one of the little beehives on the other side of the clearing. Stooping low she ducked inside and disappeared.

"What can have frightened her, I wonder?" mused the Abbess, craning her neck through the window and peering in all directions. Bridey did the same. The clearing was empty, but as they leaned out their ears caught the distant sound of jangling bridles and a long raucous laugh.

A minute passed before they saw, riding through the trees in single file, a dozen men mounted on tall horses. Bridey watched in delight as the horses shook their heads and flicked their tails, keeping wide wary eyes on the wolf-hounds which trotted panting at their heels.

The riders, talking and laughing in the afternoon sunshine, were clad in tartan. In the heat, they had cast off their fur-lined cloaks; they were startling in their finery. Large silver brooches sparkled on their bright tunics, and around their wrists were bracelets of copper and bronze. Their long hair was elaborately braided, or swept back from their brows and held by combs before it fell shining onto their shoulders. On their strong fingers glinted rings set with coloured glass and precious stones, and around their waists were belts of soft leather, fastened with buckles of gold. Their faces were haughty, with long moustaches and pointed beards, neatly combed: they looked like the embroidered figures in the long tapestry on the sanctuary wall – beautiful, arrogant horsemen in a dark wood, pursuing a ghostly white stag. But these horsemen were alive, not the lifeless figures in a frieze, and Bridey's stomach swooped as she watched.

"Who are they?" she whispered.

"Who else but the King's men would ride past so proudly?" replied the Abbess, pursing her lips. "Something is afoot in the kingdom, if the King's men are abroad – I sensed it in the sticks, though the meaning was cloudy. Something is stirring, of that there is no doubt," and as the men passed from view among the ancient oak trees, Fionnuala began to gather up the sticks and toss them again onto the cloth.

Bridey watched until the last rider vanished among the green shadows of the grove. Behind her the Abbess's wrinkled hands caressed and rearranged the sacred sticks, and Bridey listened to her murmured words:

"I am the Oak and the lightning that blasts it. I am the Giant who wields a sharp sword. I am the Queen of Hives and the salmon in a dark pool . . ."

"Mother," she ventured.

"Mmm? Are you still here, Bridey?" The Abbess looked up absent-mindedly.

"What do they say? Why do the men ride by?"

The Abbess sighed, scratching her head and gazing at the sticks where they lay on the cloth, black against the white.

"They speak of the Ancient Ones, child, though I don't understand why they should. Now is not the time for their return."

"The Ancient Ones?"

"The Tuatha dé Danaan, the greatest queens and kings of the land, the ones who lie in the barrows to the east," and the Abbess smiled as if she saw something that Bridey could not. But Bridey knew of whom she spoke. How often had her own grandmother soothed her with stories, consoling her after family feuds with tales of the olden days, tales of the Tuatha dé Danaan.

They had been a nation of brave warriors and skilful poets who dwelled in circular hilltop fortresses thousands of years ago, when Erin was a young land. Their yellow hair was worn in long curls about their shoulders, and their faces were tattooed with spiralling lines of woad that terrified their enemies and sent them screaming. Greatest among their warriors was

22

Brigit, daughter of the Dagda and bright as a flame. Fighter and musician, she was as skilled with the harp as with the sword; she could heal as swiftly as she could kill.

The Tuatha dé Danaan and their magicians ruled for seven hundred years, their reign beginning on Beltine and ending on Beltine when the Sons of Mil, with new and deadly magic, sent them defeated forever back to their tombs in the marshes. Now they were never seen, except as ghostly figures in the dreams of frightened people, or in the fires of Samain, when the old year gave way to the new.

"But what can it mean?" Bridey repeated, staring at the sticks but seeing only a meaningless jumble. "The Tuatha are from long ago; these men are from now. Where are they going?"

"I cannot tell, child," said the Abbess. "Perhaps the secret lies in the songs. Now, run along, for I've much to do. And before you go, I have remembered the errand. I need you to fetch some more inks from the wood – more blue and more red – Tahan will know what to give you. It won't take a minute."

"I'm pleased to do it," Bridey assured her. Anything was better than going back to the endless baskets.

She closed the heavy door and walked slowly across the clearing. The woman was back, nervously tending the fire. She smiled and waved, but Bridey was deep in thought, and did not look up. Her mind was full of the men on their graceful horses and in her ears she still heard the chiming of harness and the soft sound of hooves among the leaves. She longed to run after them, to duck behind a tree and watch them ride away on their beautiful horses. Perhaps one of them would turn and see her and beckon her forward. Would she run away? No, she was certain she would not. Instead she would walk towards them, as proud and haughty as could be, and the King's captain would bend and hold out a strong hand to help her up onto the back of his tall horse. They would ride away through the echoing wood, on and on until . . .

Bridey laughed and shrugged at her daydream: she was too old for such nonsense. Anyway, if she ever rode one of those horses, it would not be behind a King's man, but on her own – alone through the woods, wild and reckless.

Tahan the Greek lived in a hut deep in the oak woods at the end of a narrow winding path. The undergrowth here was thick and the old trees dense with creepers and infested with spiders; at night the air was loud with owls and squeaking bats. The people from the settlement stayed away from the woods after dark, and even in the late afternoon Bridey cast apprehensive looks to either side.

Tahan's hut was a small, turf-covered mound, with two round windows and a hole for the chimney. But no smoke came from the chimney today and the glade in which the hut stood was deserted. Only the bees hummed quietly, travelling to and from the squat wooden boxes that stood on the grass. Bridey looked about her, then went and poked her head in at the door.

"Tahan?"

There was no reply, and the door swung open to reveal a room cluttered with articles so cobwebbed and covered with leaves that this might as easily have been the lair of an animal as the home of a man. From the roof hung a multitude of ancient wreaths, their leaves dried and cracked with age. Around the walls hung parchments scrawled with strange diagrams and patterns, and in one corner a huge ball of mistletoe lay on top of a pile of musty sacks. On the table, which was a simple slab of oak, were many clay pots and bowls of strange eastern origin, bright with enamel and full of dark-coloured powders. Beside them stood a massive pestle and mortar, at the bottom of which were some half-ground berries and a fragment of dried bark. The only clean thing in the hut was a golden sickle that hung above the door, sharp and polished and gleaming.

Though deeply curious, Bridey dared not gaze for too long, for the home of a druid was not for her eyes: maybe the Abbess or the convent women would be allowed in here, but no one else. So she closed the door and went over to a rotten log and sat down to wait. Tahan arrived shortly, humming a tune and beating time on a small drum which hung round his neck. Bridey got up and greeted him and he smiled in recognition.

"Good day to you, willow-woman," he said. "I trust the weaving goes well, that your baskets are strong, and that the . . . that the willows prosper on the shore."

"Yes, thank you," said Bridey politely, and looked at her feet. Tahan's wet lips and tangled beard filled her with distaste and brought back all her earlier feelings of annoyance. There was something about his voice that maddened her – a gravelly slowness that reminded her of her own occasional stammer. He was as old as her grandmother – or older, for his hair, shaven at the front, was a dirty white about his shoulders, and his eyes, once black and snapping, were now filmed with milk. The few teeth he had were no more than brown stumps, and he had to put his food into the mortar and pound it to a pulp before he ate it.

"Why do you come to the woods on this lovely day?" Tahan was asking in the voice he would use to a child. "Is it to gather flowers, perhaps, or to learn the wisdom of the birds? Or perhaps you come bringing a new herb-basket for old Tahan?"

"Well, no, Master," mumbled Bridey, flushing in embarrassment. She should have brought the old man some food – something as a token of respect – but her mind was all over the place today.

"Do you want anything, or were you merely passing? I cannot stop to converse, my child, for it is less than ten days to Midsummer and there is much to be done. The trees are restive and they fill my head with their whispering."

"No, I came for the inks you have prepared for the convent. Mother Abbess asks if they are ready, and begs you for some more of the blue and red." She spoke with exaggerated courtesy.

Tahan looked puzzled for a moment and then went into his hut. There was more muttering and the sound of a pot falling to the earthen floor.

"Here you are, little willow-wand, here is more of the

powder that Fionnuala needs. Be careful not to spill it, it took
me many hours to prepare. Be so kind as to give Fionnuala my
greetings this fine day, and tell her that any time she cares to
take a walk in the woods I would be honoured to share her
company."

Tahan and the Abbess were friends of long-standing, having
first met when Tahan, a shy young man, had decided to end his
travels and settle down. He was already well-versed in unwrit-
ten lore and yet, he said, he still had much to learn from the
young woman at St. Brigit's convent. Friendship developed
over the years, and now the Abbess still liked to come into the
woods to walk with the druid, as they debated earnestly the
deep mysterious nature of trees, or the secrets of rhyme and
metre.

"Yes, surely, I'll tell her," said Bridey, holding out her hand
for the little packets of powder that the old man had wrapped in
fragments of deerskin, and cringing at his touch. "Good
afternoon, Master, and many thanks," and she turned and
started back along the winding path through the woods,
hurrying to get away from the old druid and the lonely clearing.

By the time she was back at the settlement the light was already
fading and she walked along dreamily, rejoicing in the glow of
the summer twilight.

Eadha was yawning in the corner, but he stumbled sleepily
over to his sister and managed to taunt, "I'm still not telling
you, Bridey; you still don't know my secret." Bridey laughed
and shooed him off to bed.

Mechanically she set about her evening chores – feeding the
geese, bringing water for the oxen, milking their small cow.
Sorcha was out, so all the work was left to Bridey. Tonight she
did not mind, and she swung through her tasks quickly. As
night began to fall a weariness settled about her shoulders and
she felt the familiar ache of a day's hard work.

She shut the door and took a last look at the settlement, the
surrounding fields and the distant gleaming lake. It was all so
familiar and safe, peacefully shrouded in darkness. Surely

nothing could disturb the quiet life of this place. But she remembered the harsh laughter of the horse-riders in the grove, and a slight shadow passed for an instant through her sleepy mind. She shrugged and waved away the uneasy feeling. Taking a candle she began to get ready for bed.

3. the golden crown

I am the wide flood on the plain ...

The next week was busy, with every spare minute spent weaving the wicker into baskets of all shapes and sizes – baskets for babies and bread, for fishing and washing, for storage or for mere decoration. At night Bridey dreamed of supple strips of willow and of her calloused fingers weaving the wet stuff – in, out, in, out – until she woke in the morning no more refreshed than when she had gone to bed. But by the end of the week most of the work was finished and Sorcha was departing for the next settlement with Cron, who looked ridiculous beneath the towering load.

Bridey walked with her some of the way, carrying on her back a creaking collection of baskets for the convent women. The day was chilly, the sky cloudy and threatening rain, and both girls wore warm cloaks belted round the waist. They talked as they walked.

"... and you look after our mother," Sorcha was saying. "She's tired by this hard work, and it's no help if you keep wandering off leaving her with everything to do. I've had my time of hard work and I'm going to enjoy myself before it's too late."

"Before it's too late!" said Bridey. "You mean before you get married."

"That's none of your business," said Sorcha primly. "Don't you be gossiping to our mother or ... "

"Or what?" snapped Bridey, irritated. Why must Sorcha fuss so?

"Or I'll take back the coracle."

Bridey shrugged. It was no good arguing; her sisters were older. But they were stupid too, with their giggling and flirting and the way they whispered behind their hands in front of men. She didn't see the point. She decided never to marry.

They said goodbye at the crossroads and Bridey took the right hand turning for the convent. There was no one about when she reached the clearing, so she left the baskets in the shelter of the refectory and started for home, taking the wide road that led to the settlement, for it was too damp and windy to cross the marshes. Half-way back the rain came down, turning the path to mud, and Bridey tramped miserably on, her hood pulled down around her face and the cold mud squeezing up inside her shoes.

Back at the settlement there was a good deal of activity despite the steady rain. A crowd of people had gathered and now stood together with squares of sacking held above their heads, talking animatedly. As Bridey walked through the gate she saw more people running from the circle of huts that stood within the fence. In the midst of the crowd, holding his restless horse by the reins, a man stood with water dripping off the end of his nose. His fur-lined cloak was dark with rain and his eyes wandered across the crowd with a mocking stare.

"Who is he?" Bridey asked the woman who stood next to her. It was Ailinn, her mother's cousin – a small, frail person, but strong-minded and with a caustic tongue. She laughed humourlessly.

"A messenger from the King, so he says, though he doesn't look so smart with his beard uncurled and his fur all limp and sorry-looking." She gave a chuckle and whispered confidentially, "They think they're so grand, with their big horses and their shiny swords, but everyone knows it's so much foolishness. Why don't they find something useful to do, instead of riding round shouting and trampling over everyone's fields?" Her face was serious; she looked as if she hated this proud-looking messenger.

"What does he say?" Bridey asked. "Has he brought news?"

"Oh, yes," said the woman, "he's brought news. He tells us

that we have a new King, for all the difference it will make. One pretty warlord is very much like another, I'd say," and she no longer masked her bitterness. Ailinn was old enough to remember the wars that had torn the land over twenty years ago, and she hated the sight of the proud rider and the way the children cheered and clapped their hands.

Bridey didn't know what to think. She couldn't imagine a real battle, with fighting that left people dead and maimed, with their farms burned and their homes destroyed: it was something that struck her as impossible, and yet she knew that it had happened. But not in her time – not in this safe marshland, miles from the border. Battles for her were still beautiful pageants where men fought bravely but were never hurt, where deeds of heroism were as common as poppies in a cornfield. In the songs of the poets warfare was glorious.

" ... and so King Eurys of the Blood-stained Sword has handed his crown to another, with the good reason that while out hunting an accident befell him whereby his brave left hand, which was as fair and as strong as a falcon's talon, was grievously mauled by a ravening boar. No longer unblemished was our good King and so, by ancient law and most sacred creed, abdicate he must, or suffer death from the hands of his men ... " The King's messenger was repeating his proclamation in a bored voice; he sounded weary and irritated, as if he scorned the dripping crowd that stood before him, hanging on his words. He smoothed his fur cuffs and continued.

"And now our King, who shall be known as Breagh of the New Hand, with Lir, Prince of Killala, does most nobly call upon you, his people, to join with him in quelling the impudent trespasses of our neighbour, High King Niall of Tara, whose foul deeds are laying waste our kingdom and whose tribute, if paid, would empty our coffers and leave our children to starve. Your King needs brave men. A gold coin for all who fight."

The proclamation ended abruptly and there was a surprised silence. The messenger jumped up onto his wet horse and prepared to ride away.

"Remember," he called, flinging back his cloak, "a gold coin for all who gather at Cruachan within the month," and he tightened his reins and kicked with his heels. The horse sprang away and the crowd watched as he cantered steadily off through the stockade gates and disappeared in the direction of the neighbouring settlement. Everyone had started speaking at once:

"By the Saint, what a languid fellow mi-laddie is!" joked one.

"To be sure," agreed a second, "too much trouble to open his mouth, almost!"

"Well, I think it's a shame," a woman cried. "What need the old fool step down, just because he hurt his hand on a boar?"

"And what about this new one? What rashness is this, to fight our neighbours?" An old woman sighed and shook her head. "This Breagh sounds a rash and ruthless fool."

"Isn't he that half-wit cousin of Eurys?"

"Certainly he's weak in the wits if he wants us to fight the High King, and with the harvest nearly ready, too!"

"And that Prince Lir is no more than a baby! Our taxes pay for too many arrogant princelings."

"Gutless cowards!" came a loud voice. "Those wretches have been filching our cattle and horses long enough. Put a stop to it, that's what I say." It was the wheelwright who spoke, and his words drowned out everyone else. "Why should we be squeezed to death by greedy Tarans? What right do they have to steal from us?"

"Oh, get away, you know we do the same to them, 'tis well understood. What's a few ponies between friends? We do good trade with them. Who needs a war?" Feargal, another cousin of Bridey's, gave a jeering laugh.

"And what if you got caught with your breeches down by a pack of heathen Yellow-Hairs in a long ship?" replied the wheelwright mockingly. "Then you'd go running to your King soon enough, I warrant, crying for his warlords to help you, you ungrateful dog! Yet you refuse to fight when he needs you."

"I'm no traitor," asserted the first man, "but nor am I a fool."

31

"Coward, then," called the wheelwright.

The two men advanced threateningly, chins stuck out and eyes goggling. They stared furiously for a few seconds before lunging at one another, fists smacking against each other's face and body. Bridey felt her stomach tighten, but almost at once the men were pulled apart by Gegra and Dian – not before the wheelwright's nose had been split and Feargal's tunic ripped in three places.

Ailinn barged forward and confronted the two red-faced men.

"Are you mad!" she cried. "Do you become two little boys again so easily? A few silky words from a dandified messenger and you're at each other's throats. You make me sick!" and she spat disgustedly on the ground. Feargal and the wheelwright pushed past her indifferently, and the wheelwright's loud voice could be heard as he made his way through the crowd:

" . . . a bunch of sentimental fools, you lot, scared of a bit of bloodshed. What are they but a bunch of dirty Tarans, after all . . . "

Bridey shivered. Until now the Tarans had been legendary enemies of Connacht, glittering and brave, who dwelt in the songs and ballads of the poets, and skirmished with their neighbours across the flat bog-lands of the east. Now they were dirty and threatening, and she prepared herself to hate them. Rain began to trickle down the back of her neck and as she turned to go she caught sight of the Abbess, standing alone as the crowd dispersed, and she splashed over the sodden grass towards her.

"Mother," she said, "will there be a war? Is that what the sticks were saying? Is that why the King's men were riding by?"

"I don't know, Bridey," the Abbess shrugged. "There will always be war. It's only a matter of time. Perhaps we have no choice in it at all." She looked sad and angry. "Certainly there are changes afoot. A King must step down if any flaw or blemish appears on his body. There are many things a King must avoid, many rituals he must observe, and I pray to Our Lady that this Breagh New Hand has good counsel."

"What rituals?"

"Oh, my dear, so many, I cannot keep up with them. Let me see," the Abbess narrowed her eyes, "a King may not camp for nine days or nights upon the plain of Cualaan, or travel the Duibhlinn road on a Monday; he may not ride a spotted steed on the heath of Dal Chais, or a black-heeled mare across Magh Maistean . . . " Her voice trailed off and she looked up at the rain-soaked clouds. "But what good does it do," she murmured, "when a King makes all observance and yet leads his people to their death?"

Bridey said nothing. It all seemed so far away, this talk of Kings and battlefields.

"Perhaps Liadan can help me read the sticks," muttered the Abbess to herself. "Maybe she can read the signs more easily."

Bridey watched Fionnuala walk briskly over the grass towards the road that led to the convent. She did not follow, but instead turned and ran home, where she huddled by the fire with her tunic steaming about her knees, and thought of what the Abbess had said. She remembered the King's men and their horses, and the sneering voice of the messenger; then thought with excitement of Liadan, chief bard of Connacht, who was bringing her court to the settlement this Midsummer week.

Listening to the fire spit and crackle and feeling its warmth, Bridey's head began to nod. She could hear her mother moving about, muttering about the King's messenger. With her mind full of kings and fragments of verse, Bridey fell asleep.

She was woken by Eadha rushing in and banging the door behind him. His wet hair was stuck to his face and he was flushed with excitement. He had been fishing with his friends and now he proudly laid on the table three fat, speckled trout.

"Look!" he cried. "I caught them all by myself."

Bridey rubbed her eyes and yawned; for a second she was unsure where she was, and she watched her brother as he stroked the glistening fish. Her mind was still muddled with dreams – a pool of blood, and the sound of screaming, soldiers running, the smell of burning and the incessant bang of a drum . . . She looked at Eadha and shook her head to clear her

33

thoughts. She saw him dead, his bones crushed beneath the hooves of a galloping horse, and she felt a sudden stab of loss.

Eadha smiled and stroked his fish.

"I killed them all on my own, you know. No one helped."

Bridey swallowed and licked her lips.

"Well done," she remarked in a dry voice, but she was filled with distaste at the bruised fish and their gaping bloodied mouths.

"Can I have a ride in the coracle now?" piped the boy.

Bridey would have dismissed him again. She was feeling too tired to move, confused and sickened by her nightmare – she would give him a turn tomorrow. But as she looked at his eager face she relented: after all, it was not such an effort, and it would give him pleasure.

"Come on, then," she said, rising heavily from her chair. "Just for an hour, now. Is it still raining?"

Eadha shouted for joy and clapped his hands. The sun was just about to come out, he assured her, the rain was light. Look – he was hardly wet at all!

After an hour they were both soaked. Eadha had fallen in twice and Bridey had anxiously dived in after him, though she knew he was a strong swimmer. She was unaccountably protective of him today. Now she sat on the bank shivering, watching as he steered the boat to and fro on the lake. The flat grey water was etched with silver circles where the raindrops fell, and the shores of the lake were lost in mist.

"Come in now," she called hoarsely, wiping the rain from her eyes, and she drew her sodden cloak more tightly around her. When Eadha finally pulled the coracle up on the bank, he was delirious with excitement.

"When can I do it again?" he asked.

"Not till I say so," replied Bridey firmly. "Next week, perhaps."

Eadha's face fell, but he held his tongue and followed his sister back towards the settlement, carrying one side of the wet coracle. When they were inside the gates, Bridey said, "Well now, what about your secret?"

Eadha looked up in surprise. How could he have forgotten? It had been almost impossible keeping silent all week. But now he could tell. Now he could show Bridey what he had found.

"It's in the cow-shed," he said, and dropping his side of the coracle where he stood, he rushed off towards the turf building. Bridey sighed, picked up the coracle, and followed him.

She found him searching in a pile of straw at the far end of the shed. The cows watched, chewing impassively, and as Bridey took off her cloak, Eadha produced something wrapped in a floury sack. With ceremony he held the sack aloft.

"Here it is," he whispered solemnly.

Bridey waited, squeezing water from her hair. She was dreaming of supper and she watched without interest while Eadha fumbled with the sack. But as he threw it to one side and raised his hands triumphantly, she sat up, gasping with astonishment. She had expected an old shoe, a dead fox, something useless. Nothing like this.

It was a golden crown. Not shiny and new like a king would wear, but an old battered circle of stained and tarnished gold, dented and dull with age, and as Bridey knelt forward to examine it more closely, she saw that it was decorated with fine engravings, intricate spirals that whirled round and round, confusing the eye. Empty sockets showed where the jewels had been.

"Oh!" she exclaimed. "Where did you find it?"

"Down by the lake," said Eadha triumphantly, "among the reeds – just lying there as if someone had thrown it away. So I took it."

"I wonder whose it is?"

Eadha frowned. "It's mine, of course."

"No, I mean I wonder whose it *really* is."

Eadha looked sulky.

"I found it," he muttered, looking down.

"Yes, but you can't keep it," said Bridey. "It's old, it may be valuable. It must belong to someone."

"No, it doesn't," insisted the boy.

"Well, what do you want it for?" asked Bridey scornfully.

"For my head, of course," said Eadha, and he put it on. It fell comically over one ear and across his brow, and he squinted up at his sister ruefully. But Bridey did not laugh.

"Give it to me," she said, and she tried on the crown herself.

It fitted, and Bridey's hands caressed it where it rested lightly on her wet head. This was not a king's crown, she thought excitedly, tracing the spirals, it had belonged instead to a queen, a warrior queen. Perhaps she had been one of the Tuatha dé Danaan, and had led her people into battle stained from head to foot with woad, her yellow hair streaming from below her crown.

"Give it back," said Eadha. "It's mine," and he narrowed his eyes as he stared at the circle of gold.

"Listen. It's not yours any more than it's mine," retorted Bridey, suddenly angry. "You only found it, and it doesn't even fit you. I'll make a bargain: you can have the boat, if I can have the crown." She was surprised at her strong feeling of possession, and the careless way she gave up her treasured coracle. She took off the crown and stroked the old metal, looking at the spiralling patterns. "It's mine now, Eadha, do you hear me?"

The boy looked at his sister sullenly, but he saw a cold gleam in her eye that meant he should not protest. He was in a quandry: he wanted the coracle but he did not want to lose the crown. With ill-grace he nodded his head.

"Very well," he said, and shoulders drooping he left the warm cow-shed and went back outside into the rain.

4. Líaòan's court

I am the wind on deep water ...

Three days passed and the weather recovered, but Bridey never regained the happiness she had felt the day she spent collecting willow in her coracle. It was as if the serenity she achieved that day – her enjoyment of the little boat, the daydreams about the King's men – had all been an illusion. Now she hated her family, hated everyone in the settlement, hated their poverty and their incessant labour. She busied herself with her baskets, gritting her teeth in irritation if anyone came near.

Every hour dragged, and although the sun shone and the lake was like a mirror, Bridey felt none of her usual pleasure. She shunned the company of her friends and sent Eadha away with cruel words. If her mother tried to comfort her, she ran off down to the marshes where she stared sightlessly at the gnats as they danced above the hollow rattling reeds.

"What's the use?" she asked herself when she saw the people gathering wood for the Midsummer fires. "Don't they see how pointless it all is?" She wandered along in the wake of the rumbling carts, ducking behind trees and kicking her feet in the leaves, surprised at the harshness of her thoughts. If anyone said hello she turned away, anxious to be alone – but ready to cry from loneliness. She had no real friends, no one she could speak to about her depression, or about the nightmares which troubled her imagination. She was unloved, and yet if anyone expressed affection she recoiled, silent and embarrassed.

She had taken the golden crown from the stable and hidden

it among the roots of a willow, and every morning, after milking the cow, she would take the coracle across the lake to check that her prize was still there. If Eadha minded, he dared not speak; these days Bridey frightened him. Anyway, for the rest of the day the coracle was his, for his own adventures.

Bridey did not especially like the crown. It was ugly and sinister and sat ominously in her hand, the empty sockets dull and lustreless. But when she put it on her head, she felt reassured. Then it seemed beautiful after all, as it had been when she first saw it. And yet what could it be, this strange feeling that would not go away? It was as if she had an itch that she could not find, tickling somewhere inside her mind; as if she had unfinished business, or had put something down and now could not find it. When she took off the crown and pushed it back into its hiding place, these feelings did not go away. Instead she felt her frustration increase until it was almost unbearable, and she swore at the leaky coracle as it drifted erratically over the lake. Narrowing her eyes, she would gaze at the line of fast water where the current flowed. If she let herself drift, she would soon be tugged irrevocably towards the centre, and then it would be a matter of seconds before she was pulled into the relentless current and carried away south. Oh, how delightful it would be, how quick . . .

Bridey gave a jump and found herself hot and sweating with the coracle dangerously far out. Pulling hard on her paddle she steered for the shore, flushed with shame. What was she thinking of? She pulled the boat through the water, wondering what it could be that so preoccupied her. What had happened to make her so irritable and unkind?

As she walked back to the village, she met the carts returning from the woods, loaded with oak-wood for the fires. As usual Tahan the Greek was organising everyone, getting in the way as he directed operations in his laborious, quavering fashion, and Bridey looked at him in disgust. As she turned away she was hailed by one of the boys who came running up with a broad smile on his face. It was Cormac, the bee-keeper's son, his curly hair full of oak-leaves.

"Bridey! Where have you been hiding? What's the matter? Are you ill?"

Bridey cringed, but could not escape. It was not that she did not like Cormac – they were good friends, and had been so ever since childhood when Cormac, a year older than Bridey, had taught her how to use a slingshot. They had spent whole days exploring the marshes together. Now that they were grown and had to work, they were less adventurous, but would still snatch moments away to roam in the marshes again. But today Bridey was annoyed by Cormac's friendliness and good humour, and she shook her head and turned away, mumbling an excuse. Or an insult – Cormac could not quite catch it.

"Bridey, wait . . ." he tugged at her sleeve. "Are you coming? The poets are here and the Abbess is going to greet Liadan. We're going to watch." He spoke excitedly and pointed back at a group of friends who, with sprigs of oak in their hair, were making their way through the woods towards the convent.

"Oh, get your hands off!" snarled Bridey as she whirled away, her skin on fire where he had brushed her. "Don't you dare touch me, you idiot!"

Cormac's face lost its smile as he stepped back in surprise, hurt and angry.

"Very well," he said coldly. "Stay by yourself and keep your own miserable company. But don't come running to me when *everybody* hates you!" And he turned and strode away towards the other young people. Bridey could hear his laughter, loud and forced, echoing through the trees, and a sharp pain in her chest made her draw breath and blink her eyes. She wished she could call to him; wished she could run after him and join the others.

She slunk back behind the bole of the tree and hid, watching the last of the carts roll away towards the settlement. Last of all went Tahan the Greek, chuckling and murmuring to himself and tapping his crooked fingers lightly on his drum. As he vanished through the trees Bridey came out and started following slowly and miserably in the direction of the convent. Her eyes were on the ground but she did not see the brown leaves and pools of sunlight. Through her mind passed a glorious cavalcade: a line of proud and noble men mounted on tall high-stepping horses, with sharp iron swords at their sides. They were brave and beautiful, cantering off to war. Her feeling of loneliness deepened.

Liadan of Corkaguiney visited the convent whenever she could. Abbess Fionnuala was learned in the art of poetry, having studied with Liadan, and although she was not a full bard, she knew many of the long, intricate poems and would recite them on winter evenings round the fire, or on summer nights under the stars. She knew much of the ancient ritual and her harp-playing was of renown. All the convents of St. Brigit were centres of learning and poetry, for Brigit was the blessed Muse from whom springs all inspiration: the patron saint of bards, and their invincible protector.

Bridey had grown up surrounded by poetry and song, and never an evening passed without someone standing to sing or recite a few lines of verse. But Bridey never sang herself because she was scared of being laughed at for her stammer, and she kept her songs for when she was alone in the woods or out on the lake in the coracle. Everyone sang, but the secrets and magic of the poets were unknown to the singers: only the bards knew of those.

Many said that Liadan was the greatest poet alive. There was none to equal her in the land of Connacht, nor perhaps in the whole of Erin itself; not even at the table of the King. Stories of her prowess and her power abounded – the beauty of her voice was matchless. Even Bridey, lonely and disconsolate as she was, could not stop a thrill of excitement at the thought of catching sight of this greatest of poets. She quickened her pace, stepping over the deep ruts left in the forest floor by the returning carts. Branching off towards the convent she was soon within sight of the clearing.

It was crowded with people, and in the middle of the crowd stood the Abbess, her arms outflung as she admonished the onlookers, shouting at the boys and men to stand back, telling

the women to sit down in an orderly line. The men were to go
back below the trees, for they were not allowed any nearer the
convent, and they retreated sheepishly and clustered in the
shade, peering over each other's shoulders. Bridey could see
Eadha standing at the front with his friends, his head twisting
to and fro. Cormac was nearby, smiling genially, his arm
thrown around the neck of Bres the swineherd.

"Do you want to shame me?" the Abbess was shouting.
"Keep quiet, now, or by St. Brigit I'll get Liadan to speak such
a verse as will make your voices squeak like chickens." The
people quietened. Liadan was known to have such a merciless
command of satire that she could cause boils to break out on a
man's face, or turn his bowels to water with a few simple lines.

As the giggling died down nothing could be heard but the
wind in the trees; then, one by one, heads turned at the sound
of bells, faint and tuneful, coming towards them through the
warm air as Liadan led her court into the clearing. Mounted on
a small grey horse, she seemed to the curious crowd somehow
more ordinary than they remembered. Perhaps they thought
she would be tall and beautiful, with flashing eyes and a perfect
face: a woman of such power must be lovely indeed. But if
anyone was disappointed, they did not show it, and they
watched in silence as Liadan trotted forward.

She was a woman of middle years, broad-shouldered and
heavy, with strong hands that gripped the reins; and the only
thing about her that was elaborate or out of the ordinary was
the brilliant cloak that fell from her shoulders, tumbling over
the grey rump of the horse. It seemed to shine with every
imaginable colour: swirling and many-hued, against a back-
ground of deep black. The onlookers in their dun-coloured
cloth sighed with pleasure at the splendour of Liadan's
embroidered mantle. It was her *tugen*, a garment only to be
worn by the greatest of bards.

The Abbess stepped forward and held out her hands.
Speaking in a loud, formal manner she greeted her guest:

"Welcome, Liadan of Corkaguiney, most skilful of
Rhymers. Oft is it said that the very birds must fall from the

trees in their envy, and the deer flee through the forest for fear of your tongue. Pray rest awhile with us and enrich us with your verse." She gave a gracious smile.

Liadan smiled and answered likewise, in formal speech, and her voice was so lilting, resonant and rich that the people in the crowd sighed again and saw that, of course, she was a beautiful woman, after all.

"I thank you, Fionnuala, much-reverenced Mother," she said. "We are in sore need of food and rest, and feign would bide in this peaceful glade until such time as we are refreshed." Looking barely tired at all, she sprang from the saddle and, formalities over, the two women clasped hands and gave each other a private smile of deep friendship.

"Come inside," said the Abbess. "It will be dark soon, but there is yet time for us to talk." She led the woman in the fine cloak towards the sanctuary. As they disappeared into the low building and pulled shut the heavy door, the rest of Liadan's court began to dismount. The convent women rushed forward to hold the horses, the poets were welcomed and food was brought.

Liadan travelled with twenty-four fellow-bards and apprentices, all of whom now strolled about on the soft grass of the clearing to stretch their legs. The convent women went to and fro with jugs of milk and mead and platters of food. The people from the settlement, watching from a distance, waited for half an hour gazing at the poets' fine clothes and handsome ponies. Bridey also lingered, watching the faces of the people in the clearing – these poets, who lived such a different life, travelling from place to place with their heads full of poetry. She wondered enviously what it must be like for them to have such power over words. A full bard knew enough poetry to be able to recite verse for several hours a day for an entire year – airs, romances, ballads ... How strange for them, she thought, to do no work; never to look for willows or sweat over baskets. These creatures, with their soft hands and their weak backs: they were no better than her, she was sure of that. A few days ago she might have held these people in awe, might have

admired their gaudy clothing and their easy words, but something had changed to make her see things differently. She was
confused. Now she almost despised them.

She was about to sneak away through the woods when her
attention was caught by one of the poets who was leading her
horse to the water-trough on the edge of the clearing. At first it
was the horse and not the girl that made Bridey turn and stare:
a small bay pony, with a sprinkling of white spots and a long
smooth tail. Its spotted face wore an intelligent expression, and
it was skipping about, annoyed at something its mistress had
done, and the young apprentice was tugging at the reins,
whispering to the restless animal.

"Shh! Quiet now, Ceibhfhionn," she said, patting the
skewbald neck. "Behave yourself. There's no need for a fuss."

Bridey disliked the girl even before she looked into her face –
disliked her for having such a pony, for being a bard and not a
basket-weaver, for knowing poetry and wearing tartan
breeches . . . But when she saw her, she exclaimed in surprise
and felt a flash of recognition. Her dislike deepened.

The girl looked like Bridey. Not exactly like, but the
similarity would surely have struck anyone who saw them
together. She had the same green eyes and black lashes, the
same slope to her nose and the same pointed chin. Pulling at the
pony's reins she glanced up and saw Bridey, and her lips parted
in a smile. As she raised her head, the hood of her cloak fell
back to reveal hair the colour of raw flax. How could anyone
have hair that colour? Hair was dark brown or black – unless
you were old, when it was streaked with grey. This girl must be
a Yellow-hair, Bridey thought as she ran through the trees, a
savage from the cold countries to the north who came in long
ships to steal and burn. What was she doing here with Liadan's
court?

Before long she stood among the alders that grew by the
marshes, trembling with a mixture of emotions. She sat down
on a damp tussock to recover. Breathing deeply she stared
across the marshes and waited for her heart to cease pounding.
A few minutes passed and the rustling of the trees and the rattle

of the reeds echoed dully through her thoughts. Then the crack of a twig caused her to turn and there, standing with her hands in her pockets and a smile upon her face, was the young bard. Bridey was lost for words.

"Good evening," said the girl. "I saw you in the woods. I wondered if you might care for a moment's conversation. Perhaps we could share a few rhymes, for we seem to share the same face," and she grinned at Bridey in a friendly fashion. It was uncanny. Apart from the different hair, Bridey felt as if she was looking at her reflection in the flat waters of the lake.

She stared speechlessly at the girl whose words were so rapid and liquid and gleeful. She spoke with the accent of the rich, the way people spoke who did not have to work hard, or wear dirty clothes, and who spent their time laughing and being clever and sneering at basket-weavers. This girl who looked so like her struck Bridey dumb, and now she felt like a clod beside the careless confidence of the bard. The girl was talking again, but Bridey stared at her feet and could not look up.

"My name's Canola. I am with Liadan of Corkaguiney – apprenticed and bound for twelve years, more's the pity," and she grimaced and laughed. "I've escaped from them because Eodain has started her preaching and I couldn't bear it any more. She's my teacher, the skinny one with the long nose. Did you see her? I made up a riddle about her once: What is as thin as a knife, full of wind and whistles when it sleeps? Do you like it? It's not very kind, I suppose, but then *she's* not very kind sometimes, so it serves her right. What's your name?"

Bridey shrugged her shoulders. Why should she talk to this girl? She hadn't sought Canola out, so why did Canola have to intrude upon her with this educated voice and husky laugh? There was an uncomfortable silence.

"Excuse me," said Canola, raising one eyebrow. "You whisper so softly, I can barely catch your words. Perhaps if you spoke up . . ."

"I-I didn't ask you to c-come after me," said Bridey, looking at her from beneath her brows. "I don't need c-company," and she winced, loathing the sound of her own voice and waiting for

44

the poet to laugh. But Canola did not seem to mind the stammering and she carried on as if she had not noticed.

"A-ha!" she said. "You see – I can hear if you bellow! But please, don't burst my ears with amiability. I've no desire to steal your solitude," and she chuckled. "Maybe the trees find you good company." She raised both eyebrows and watched Bridey with a steady gaze. Then she examined her fingernails minutely and recited:

> *Raspberry, mulberry,*
> *Blackthorn or myrtle;*
> *If only the sun*
> *Would give warmth to this damsel!*

She turned her back and started to whistle.

Bridey felt hot with anger, but there was nothing she could do. The words seemed to drip from the girl's tongue like honey from a spoon. She felt dull and tongue-tied, and though she racked her brain for a suitably cutting remark, she could think of nothing. She was inclined simply to call her names, but she knew how lame it would sound after the practised sarcasm of the bard. Anyway, Canola was a poet: she was privileged and protected; if Bridey insulted her she would get into trouble.

"Go away," she said.

"Well, well, well," laughed Canola. "I thought it was a tree-stump, but it has a tongue. A face like a poet and a tongue like a fish – a marsh-sprite, perhaps, or Banna Naomha the Trout."

"You're very c-clever," retorted Bridey loudly, "but you don't scare me. You may speak in riddles, but you impress no one b-but yourself." She battled to get the words out clearly, but the more she fought, the more tangled they became.

Canola sighed.

"I just wanted to talk," she said in an ordinary voice.

Bridey rose and brushed the leaves from her tunic. Again she looked enviously at Canola's cross-bound tartan breeches and at the great bronze buckle at her waist, and jealousy stirred in her stomach like a snake. She disliked this girl's wealth and cleverness, but looking into the green eyes that were so like her own Bridey felt a strange sensation: it was almost as if she disliked herself, as if she stared at her own reflection in the water and hated what she saw.

"Oh, g-go back to your poets and your scholars," she said. "Talk to them. Show them your b-brilliance and wit," and she pushed past Canola and stumbled back up the path.

The young poet watched her go, marvelling at such unfriendliness in a complete stranger. But she was used to being on her own, for the poets were a remote group, scornful of ordinary folk and enamoured of their own importance – it was quite usual for people to avoid them. Even among the apprentices Canola found it hard to make friends, the strange paleness of her hair set her apart. She sighed once more and started wearily back through the trees. She had a hundred lines of verse to learn, and she must rehearse her poem for Midsummer night as she had been chosen by Liadan to entertain their hosts at the feast. Eodain would be after her if she did not get back. Hitching up her trousers she disappeared into the gloom.

5. midsummer's night

I am the blaze on the hillside ...

Two days later it was Midsummer and the people of the marsh settlement gathered to celebrate. Work was put aside and the day was given over to dance, music and story-telling. Everywhere groups of people listened wide-eyed to the words of the poets. The children quickly learned to mimic the flowery speech, and they ran between the huts shouting rhymes and chasing each other until they fell exhausted onto the dry grass, and listened breathlessly as yet more stories were woven effortlessly out of the hot summer air.

Tahan the Greek moved among the people smiling mysteriously and waving a long spray of oak-leaves. His golden sickle hung from his belt and countless twigs had caught in his beard. If a group of girls paused for a second in their play, or boys stopped to giggle with their friends, he would regale them with a long lament on the death of the Oak-King, his eyes growing misty with sentiment as he warmed to his task. He did not notice the girls as they drifted off to hunt the wren, their tiny Midsummer quarry. At length the Abbess found him mumbling verses to himself in the shade of the oaks, and she took him back to the convent for a refreshing cup of elderflower. "It's a long day, Tahan, old friend," she said as she poured the wine. "Ah, yes, indeed – the very longest . . . " replied the druid wearily and drained his cup.

All through the hot afternoon people played and sang and told stories, until one by one they went home to recover, in preparation for the Midsummer feast and the night ahead. While they rested, half a mile away in the cool of the convent

47

clearing, Abbess Fionnuala was playing *fidchell* with Liadan the poet.

They talked animatedly as their hands moved the pieces over the board of yew-wood, their conversation littered with learned Latin references – Pliny, Gregory the Great and countless other authors. They were discussing the new King and the rumours of war.

"War!" declared Liadan. "*Horresco referens!* I shudder at the word!" She calmly took one of Fionnuala's pieces and smiled.

"You play aggressively today," remarked Fionnuala placidly, and made her move. Liadan exclaimed in vexation, outmanoeuvred by her friend. Then she laughed and, carelessly brushing the pieces to one side, began to set them out for another game.

"But tell me," the Abbess said, "what of this Breagh? You say you have heard rumours. What can he be thinking of, mustering a force at this time? We cannot spare them, you know. Who would be left to bring in the harvest?"

"Oh, Fionnuala, who knows what goes on in the minds of men when they get the smell of war in their nostrils? Breagh, by all accounts, is a young fool. Eurys was an old one. We are certainly worse off with this new hothead." Liadan's voice, dark and slow as autumn honey, resonated in the warm air. The Abbess nodded slowly and moved a piece into the centre of the board.

"And does he intend to lead Connacht to war?"

The bard sighed and loosened her collar. Her heavy cloak lay beside her on the bench, and she had rolled up her sleeves and pulled off her shoes against the heat.

"It's so stuffy," she said, fanning herself with her hand. "Who can think of war on such a day?"

The Abbess looked strangely at her friend.

"My people will think of war, Liadan, if you and your bards fill their heads with eloquent nonsense. With such rumours abroad we cannot take a chance on their ears being charmed by tales of heroes."

Liadan opened her eyes and looked at the Abbess, her hands above the pieces on the board.

"But Fionnuala, *arma virumque cano* . . . I sing of arms and of the hero . . . " she replied. "Do you wish me to water down my blood-verse? Are your people such fools that they cannot tell rhetoric from reality?" She moved her piece forward with a determined gesture.

Fionnuala shrugged.

"Perhaps," she said sadly, fingering a piece indecisively, "but they're not such fools that they're not fired by a good poem. Please, my friend, not too many heroics."

Liadan gave another sigh and passed her hand across her eyes.

"Very well, then, you have my word: no glorious battle-hymns tonight. We will soothe them with romance and lull them with love. But remember, my friend, I cannot banish war from men's minds, and that is where the struggle really dwells. Remember, a poet cannot carry arms."

"A poet's tongue is as lethal as a sword," remarked the Abbess drily, "and you have wounded many in your time."

"Ah, yes," replied the poet with a sidelong glance, "but my wounds give wisdom. A poet's tongue may be sharp, but the victims remain whole."

"That's handy for foolish kings!"

Liadan laughed. A companionable silence descended on the low room as the two women sat and quietly watched a shaft of dusty sunlight fall across the board and the little wooden figures.

Two miles away in the shade cast by the willows, Bridey was sitting motionless on the bank, her eyes fixed on a grey heron picking its way through the marshes nearby. She knew where its nest was, having found it the week before in a reed-bed, and now she watched its progress as if it could give her some vital information she could not find elsewhere.

Abruptly the heron rose in the air and flapped away over the lake. Bridey watched it go, then rubbed her eyes and blinked.

She had a headache from the noisy settlement and had come here in desperation; it was impossible to find any peace there today.

On her head was the golden crown, and from time to time she lifted her hands to touch it, to reassure herself that it was still there. Her mind was full of galloping horsemen in flowing cloaks, but this time she was not simply watching them ride by. Now she rode with them, galloping at their head, holding a long sword and wearing the golden crown. With one hand clenched in her horse's clammy mane and the other firmly gripping the spiralled hilt of her sword, she glanced down: the hand that held the sword was wet with blood, and a sticky crimson stained the bronze of her blade; beneath her nails was a dark rust-coloured crust. Was this her hand? Those were her fingers, strong and calloused; those were her nails, chipped from weaving the stubborn wicker. Why were they covered in blood? Whose blood was it . . . ?

Shouting with horror, Bridey jerked awake. Above her head the silver leaves whispered and sighed as the sun sank slowly across the lake. Bridey looked about her bewildered, scarcely aware of where she was, until catching sight of the coracle tethered to a root, she recalled the time and place. Stretching out her hands, she looked at them in disgust. They seemed like gnarled claws, rough from hard work and grimed with dirt. Repelled, she raised them to her temples and slowly pushed the golden crown from her head. Casting furtive looks to either side, she thrust it deep into a dark hole in the bank below her. Clambering down she lowered herself carefully into the coracle and began to row home across the darkening lake.

By midnight the fires had dwindled to piles of smouldering embers. Once in a while a shower of sparks rose in the air as a branch crashed into the glowing centre and the people turned their heads to watch. There was an air of contentment and peacefulness as they sat together in the orange glow. On the outskirts someone was playing the pipes, the mournful sound was like the wind. Though the fires had died down, the memory of them would stay in the people's minds throughout the following year, the roar and snap of the flames, the blistering heat, and the smoke that had filled the sky and blocked out the stars.

Spits had been erected over the ashes and onto these were thrust the carcasses of a sheep, a pig and an ox, and the smell of meat replaced that of smoke as the people began to feast. There was more singing and dancing, more games, until everyone was too tired to move.

Then the poetry began.

First the bard Baile rose to his feet to be greeted by loud applause. He was tall and languid, with long black hair and eyes that drooped wistfully, and his voice made people sigh and stare dreamily at the stars. "I give you a poem of love and loyalty," he cried, "a poem of skill and daring ..." and everyone settled back, loosening their belts and preparing to listen.

He sang of the suicide of Deidre, beautiful and doomed, who with her lover Naiose, was foully betrayed by the vile King Conchobar. His harp jangled and shivered as he sang of the captive Deidre who, in her anger and determination, rose to her feet in the King's speeding chariot and dashed her head against an overhanging branch ... and died rather than be ruled by a man she loathed. Flowers bloomed where her blood fell, and though stakes of yew were driven through the breasts of the lovers to keep them apart in death, the yew stakes flowered and became mighty trees that still sigh in the breeze in distant Armagh.

The people wiped their eyes, and the fires were stoked. Children stretched and yawned, then settled back to wait for the next poem.

Now Liadan stood and told a story of such humour that the audience rolled on the grass, gasping with mirth. She quacked like a duck and chattered like a blackbird, roared like a bull and honked like a goose. She created endless characters – stuttering and giggling, smirking and scolding – and her harp wheezed like a bellows and squealed like a pig. There seemed no limit to the sounds she could call forth. The verse was all nonsense, with so many twists and turns that by the time she sat down her listeners were limp with hilarity.

There were yet more poems. The long sad tale of two sisters who, separated by an evil king, died from loneliness, drowning in their own tears. The story of Cred, who vowed never to lie with a man, until flattered sufficiently by her suitor's brilliant verse. The story of Cliodna of the Tuatha dé Danaan, who flew like a bird, stealing mortal lovers from the fields of Erin. But among all the stories there was none that sang of battles or vengeance, none that dealt with heroes or warriors. Liadan had kept her word.

It was two hours after midnight when Canola stood to recite her ballad. She had heard little of what had gone before, and her hands were damp with apprehension as she unslung her harp. She knew every word, every note of her song, and could recite each of the four hundred lines without stumbling, and yet she quaked with fear. Every time it was the same: the torchlit faces, some smiling encouragement, but others appraising her as if she were no more than a side of beef. The food she had swallowed at the feast churned in her stomach and she sipped a cup of mead, hoping that it would calm her nerves.

Bridey was sitting near the edge of the circle with her shawl pulled down around her face, surrounded by the older members of the settlement. She had moved away from the other young people, and now Cormac and his friends were far away on the other side of the fire. She had neither laughed at the comical songs nor cried at the tragic ones. Her mind flashed here and there, plagued by miserable imaginings. Now she watched sourly as the flaxen-haired poet walked forward into the circle of firelight.

It was with bitterness that Bridey noted how, nervous as she was, Canola moved with a certain confidence, almost a swagger, hitching up her tartan breeches as she went. She tossed her head to shake a stray strand of hair from her face, and smiled out at the audience. In the firelight her hair looked almost white. Watching her, Bridey felt slow and stupid, with a lumbering tongue and thick ugly hands. She hated the poet for her assurance and her freakish hair.

Canola looked around smiling vaguely, her teeth clamped painfully together to stop them chattering. Always she vowed to keep her eyes forward, to let her gaze drift out of focus so the faces before her became a safe anonymous blur, but each time she made the same mistake and looked about. Her stomach heaved sickly and her mouth tasted like the bottom of an old bucket. As her eyes scanned the crowd she saw Bridey sitting a little apart from the rest, surrounded by elderly listeners and shrouded by her shawl. Without thinking Canola sent her a broad smile, so relieved was she to see even one face she recognised among the crowd.

Bridey's eyes widened with surprise. From somewhere deep inside her, beyond her bitterness and jealousy, a flash of sympathy went out to the young poet. Suddenly she knew that Canola was scared, and she let her lips curve automatically into a faint smile. For the first time that night she sat up and began to pay attention.

Canola took a deep breath and glanced beyond the circle of light to where Liadan stood with the Abbess, watching closely. She shut her eyes for an instant and was soothed by the darkness, then fixing her gaze upon the very centre of the crackling fire, she sent forth a ripple of notes from her harp and began her poem: 'Brigit's Golden Crown'.

6. the warriors

I am the shining tear of the sun ...

Bridey listened closely to the ballad, watching Canola's face as she sang of long ago, of the time when the Goddess Brigit lost her crown and war broke out. The land of Erin was ravaged by plagues and brutality, crops were burnt and children died, and the people became unable to tell enemy from friend. It was a time of great sorrow, and the audience sighed and shook their heads. Canola's voice rose and fell.

The bards tried to halt the fighting, but they were helpless – poetry died, and the people forgot how to sing. In the end they did nothing but forge the weapons of death. On the edge of the circle, the Abbess listened carefully, and Liadan smiled. Canola's verse evoked none of war's illusory glory, only its horror and wastefulness. The girl's harp shivered, leaving a trail of silver notes in the air. Brigit – warrior and poet – searched for her crown. Finally she found it. Peace returned to the land.

Within the poem were many layers of meaning, puzzling riddles and apparently nonsensical chants that ran through Bridey's mind long after Canola had stopped singing.

> *"... now I have two faces. How can it be?*
> *You look in the mirror and what do you see?*
> *Do you see* you *there, or do you see* me?*"*

The rhyme stayed with Bridey as the applause died down and she muttered it to herself as she shouldered her way through the crowd. She was unaccountably thirsty and she went to where Donagha the blacksmith was presiding over a cask of ale. As she raised the bowl to her lips she saw Canola standing nearby, and she ducked her head, embarrassed to find herself blushing. She tried to leave but was hemmed in by people wanting ale, and Canola came over and touched her arm.

"Please don't go on my account," she said. "I need a drink for my poor throat – this poetry is thirsty work." She looked at the bowl in Bridey's hand. "Perhaps you find my verse a little dry, as well?"

"N-no," stammered Bridey, once again feeling shy, "it was g-good." Glancing into Canola's face she was suddenly strangely attracted, as well as repelled; part of her excited, part of her reluctant. But still she turned to leave.

"Oh, please don't go," said Canola. "We could talk. I've had enough of poetry tonight and I'm hungry. Stay for a while."

They were the same height, probably the same age, and for a few seconds they dared study each other calmly in the firelight, before Canola began moving through the jostling crowd and Bridey found herself following. Soon they were outside the great circle of fires, in a place where only a few torches flickered. Pulling a piece of bread from her pocket, Canola sat on the ground and began to eat.

"What's your name?" she asked finally, her mouth full.

"Bridey," said Bridey, and sat down beside her, her knees slightly shaky.

"Ah, Bridey for Brigit!" exclaimed Canola. "So, did you like my poem, Bridey?"

"Yes, it was good," said Bridey slowly, then unwilling to praise Canola she added, "It was . . . very long," and immediately felt foolish. "W-what was that bit about the mirror?" she said, trying to cover her embarrassment.

"Goodness, I don't know half the meaning behind it," laughed Canola, "not yet. I simply learn the lines. In a few years I may understand, but not yet. It's all very mysterious, you know, dualities, polarities . . . "

Yes, thought Bridey furiously, too mysterious for a basket-weaver, and she started to get up, but again Canola put a hand on her arm. Bridey glared at her sullenly, wanting to stay, wanting to go; frightened of being rude to this poet who held her by the sleeve.

"Let go," she said.

"Goodness!" said Canola, and she began to quote nervously in a language Bridey had never heard. Canola was unnerved by this girl who stared at her so intensely; there was something about the grubby hands and shabby, wornout clothes that made her self-conscious. She felt glittering and frivolous beside Bridey, and unable to stop talking.

Bridey interrupted.

"So, what about the two faces in the mirror?"

"Hmm," mused Canola, "that would take some reflection," and she put the last mouthful of bread into her mouth and licked her fingers. Suddenly her voice was ordinary again.

"I wonder why we look the same?"

"Who says we do?" Bridey was annoyed. She had no desire to look like this girl, with her ridiculous hair and air of superiority. She could not use clever words or play the harp. Of course, Canola must despise her. Whatever friendliness she had felt disappeared.

"I'm going," she said, scrambling to her feet and looking back at the fires.

Canola, one eyebrow raised, said nothing, but as Bridey left she called:

> *"Look in the mirror and what do you see?*
> *If you don't like yourself, then you'll never like me."*

Watching Bridey's retreating figure, she shrugged.

"Sackbuts and fiddlesticks!" she said to herself. "That one's as highly-strung as a Taran harp!" and sadly she began to pick her teeth with her long polished nails.

"Mother Fionnuala?"

"Bridey, my dear, are you still here? I thought you'd gone home." The Abbess sighed and rubbed her tired eyes with her fingers. They were standing in the doorway of the hall, a

56

timbered building at the centre of the settlement where the people assembled on feast-days. Inside was bright light, music and dancing; outside, the glow of the dying fires. The air was chilly and the stars shone brightly.

"Mother – the p-poem that girl recited – how much of it is true?" Bridey looked intently into the old face and shifted from foot to foot, her hands clasped nervously behind her back.

"Oh, yes, the one with the pale hair. Do you know, child, she bears a striking resemblance to you."

Bridey bit her lip to keep silent, hot and embarrassed and angry at the Abbess.

"One could take you for sisters ... apart from the hair," Fionnuala mused, unaware of the effect of her words. "Very strange ... Now, what were you saying?"

"The poem – about the crown, Brigit's crown – could any of it be true?"

The Abbess looked thoughtfully at the girl.

"Well, now, Bridey; *magna est veritas*, great is truth – especially when it comes to poems. They can be many things, but one thing they are never is completely devoid of truth."

Bridey frowned into the darkness. All these words. Why couldn't people say what they meant? Canola would have understood easily enough, she thought bitterly.

"So – there could be a crown?"

"Oh, yes, of a sort. But why do you ask?"

Bridey mumbled something incoherent and excused herself. The Abbess looked up vaguely to find the girl hurrying away, so she turned back to watch the dancing.

Alone by the fire with her thoughts, Bridey sat and pondered. She was stupid to think that the old crown hidden beneath the willows could have belonged to Brigit. Brigit wasn't an ordinary mortal woman, to possess a battered old crown. She was ... There were no words for it, and Bridey lay back in the damp grass and looked up at the stars. They gleamed coldly down from a blank sky. A cold breeze blew and Bridey shivered. She felt calm and empty, and she waited for a few minutes listening to the distant music; then she yawned: it was near dawn and she suddenly longed for bed. Clambering up, she started walking slowly away from the fires.

All at once bright lights danced before her eyes and the night was full of shouting and the jangle of harness. Horsemen, their faces sharp in the torchlight, were galloping by. She felt the beat of the horses' hooves and their warmth as they passed, and smelled their sweat and the sweet crushed grass. They did not stop but rode past the fires and straight through the wide entrance of the hall. After staring for a moment, Bridey ran after them as fast as she could.

The people watched open-mouthed, some still with arms raised and toes pointed, frozen in their dancing. The pipes trailed off, discordant and squeaky. Voices died away until there was silence.

The riders did not dismount, but stayed astride their horses, keeping them tightly reigned until they tossed their heads and snorted with irritation, unnerved by the torchlight. A child called: "Who are they?" but was quickly hushed by his mother. With a shock, the people recognised the emblem on the men's tunics: the rearing horse, sign of Connacht and the King.

The captain kicked forward his horse until he stood in the very centre of the hall, and when there was complete silence he spoke:

"People of the marsh-settlement! We come from your King, Breagh of the New Hand, bringing his summons. Connacht is sorely threatened by the enemy, who roam the land destroying our homes. They hang the old folk in the trees and drown the young in the wells; no building remains standing where they pass, and flocks of carrion darken the skies. The crows are feasting on the eyes of your countrymen . . ."

His voice was strong and carried to every corner of the hall. He could have been a poet, thought the Abbess as she stood listening with one hand holding onto the wall. She felt unsteady and feared she would fall.

" . . . and yet you refuse to answer the summons. But when Connacht is overrun by these savages, when all our babies are slain, will you then take heed?" He paused, and the silence

58

screamed with unspoken fears. The onlookers stared at the man, and someone at the back of the hall giggled nervously and coughed. A child whimpered.

"We need every man, every boy. We need a mighty force to crush our foe. Assemble with us at Cruachan Hill, for it is there – at the Gateway to Hell – that we stand and fight." Wheeling his horse, he turned in the saddle and cried in a contemptuous voice, "The cowards among you may stay at home with the women!" and with that he galloped through the doors, closely followed by his five surly companions.

The silence lasted a second and then there was uproar. Women shouted and men rushed about in confusion, the noise was deafening. Bridey looked around. Everywhere people were running and colliding, children were crying and tables being overturned, so that bowls fell to the floor to be smashed among the rushes. Bridey's head was throbbing so hard that she could hardly breathe as she tried to push her way out. The people had become hysterical. The beer, the fine words, the sight of the warriors, had combined to produce a drunken fervour. The men shouted and swaggered, showing themselves and each other that they were as good as any horseman, or any fine poet. The boys cheered and fought, frantic with too much ale, desperately aping the glamour of the King's men.

"What is this madness? You fools! Look what you've become!"

It was Liadan. She had climbed onto a table and now stood surveying the crowd, her bright cloak thrown back and her eyes fierce. She seemed more self-possessed than ever. One by one the people turned to listen.

"Wait! Consider!" she called in her deep voice, flexing her strong hands. "Who is this King that he can call you away from your homes like this? Does this place mean so little to you? Is your manhood so *fragile* that it must respond to such a challenge? What of the fields? What of your children?"

"But our King needs us!"

"They're killing our people!"

"The filthy Tarans!" said the wheelwright.

Now the Abbess stood by Liadan. They stood together, watching the crowd.

"You should listen to Liadan, my people," cried the Abbess. "You should listen closely to her words, because she knows about these things. She is privy to the minds of kings."

"What does a poet know about war?"

"Or a woman?"

A nasty silence was followed by harsh voices that mocked the two women, and Bridey, crushed against the wall at the other end of the hall, felt sick. A few yards away, surrounded by jeering men, she saw Canola, her face pale and her mouth tightly closed. Suddenly Bridey needed to be near her, as if a string, attaching them to each other, was being drawn in. She heaved against the crush but could make no impression on the wall of heavy bodies. A familiar querulous voice could be heard nearby:

"Make way, make way you stupid fools! Get out of my way, now!"

The crowd parted, pushing Bridey further back, and Tahan the Greek limped slowly to the centre of the hall. At length he stood beside the table.

"I won't get up, Fionnuala, my dear," he said. "I feel a little stiffness in my hip tonight," and he rapped on the table with his stick, surveying the excited crowd with bleary eyes.

"Listen to me," he called, his voice shrill. "Have you forgotten? It is Midsummer night, the shortest night. How can such madness be taking place? Have you all lost your wits? Tonight is for singing and dancing. Tonight the Oak-King dies, and tomorrow he rises again to bring life back to the earth. So, what is this talk of blood and burning? Please remember ..." but his tremulous voice was swallowed up in the noise of a crowd who had had enough of words.

Bridey saw a gap and squeezed through, and was soon standing beside Canola.

"Come with me," she said, and she took the poet's hand. Pulling Canola after her, she managed to push through the people and out into the cool air. The stars had gone and the sky was streaked with grey. It was dawn, and already men were leading fat farm ponies out of their stalls, running around in search of old weapons, banging nails into ugly clubs, calling excitedly to one another. It was as if a drug had been put into their beer, they seemed so different. Could the handsome riders really have done all this?

There was Bres the swineherd, with his father. His face was flushed and his eyes rolled wildly as he clapped his hands and crowed like a rooster. Bridey had seen him earlier, listening spellbound to a ballad sung by Eodain, his thin face calm in the firelight. Now he looked mad. Cormac was beside him, his gentle face red with excitement, his voice high and piping. He too had changed. His jaw was thrust out, his eyes were wide and his forehead was beaded with sweat. Bridey looked at him and was frightened. Gegra and Dian the shepherds were standing nearby, saddling their ponies. In the eerie light they looked almost blind. Their eyes were blank and they looked through Bridey, not seeing her. She had known them all her life, but now she hardly recognised them: the men she knew were gone. More people poured out of the hall and ran through the settlement.

"What's happening?" she asked in bewilderment.

Canola was right behind her.

"They've all gone mad!" she said, echoing Bridey's thoughts. "Have they never seen a soldier before, that they get so over-excited?"

Bridey remembered the King's men, with their sharp, careless faces and mocking eyes. How could these idiots hope to follow such warriors? It was almost funny.

"They can't go!" she declared. "They can't even fight. What can they be thinking of? They're not soldiers."

Canola shrugged and pulled Bridey out of the path of a cantering pony.

"I suppose they'll die as well as any war-lord," she said. "Common blood is as red as a warrior's – and that's all that's needed."

Bridey looked down at her hands in the grey light and

remembered the warmth, the stickiness ... she wiped them quickly on her tunic.

"I don't want to watch," she said heavily, and wandered away. She could see Sorcha laughing with Bres, holding the reins of his pony, and nearby Eadha and his friends ran about, delighted by all the activity. All she wanted now was to find her bed and go to sleep. It was like a nightmare ...

"Can I come too?" said Canola, following. "I've no desire to be near them either."

Bridey said nothing but let Canola come with her. She too dreaded being alone. As the sun rose above the peaceful lake, the two girls walked away. When the early mist cleared they were not awake to see the men ride off, or the tired, confused faces of those they left behind.

7. east and west

I am the hawk on the clifftop . . .

Over the next few days the people began to realise what had happened. Wives and mothers who had cheered their men off to war started to worry, though none would admit it. If any woman dared question or criticise, she was silenced, then shunned and left to cry in private. But sometimes, as they fed their children, or kneaded dough, or threw down hay for the cows, the women wondered what had got into them to let their lives be so altered by the whims of a King they had never even seen.

More men left every day. They seemed to become nervous and uncertain at home with the women and children, almost as if they had ceased to be real men at all, and at last – some eager, some regretful – they would saddle up and ride off through the woods, calling in brave voices to the women who watched them go. Now the settlement had a sad, abandoned air, and the children played loud war-games in the dusty summer stillness.

This was Duir, the month of the Oak, when brilliant sunshine was followed by days of steady rain, and the people were busy in the fields hoeing and weeding and scaring the birds from the ripening crops. It seemed impossible that there could be a war while the settlement and its surrounding fields lay safe and quiet beside the lake.

Bridey and Canola began to spend every spare minute together. They were shy and tentative at first, but as the days passed each girl felt her reserve loosening, and they started to look forward to the next time they could get away from their duties and see each other.

Bridey was busy with her baskets and there was extra work in the fields, but whenever she could she would run to the convent clearing to find Canola. She still kept apart from her other friends, and they kept apart from her, but she could not stay away from the fair-haired poet. As she wove the wicker to make baskets, or trimmed the edges of a mat, she thought of Canola's elegant gestures and the confidence of her words. Although she envied the poet her position and her soft hands, she also began to admire her, and she liked to watch as Canola raised her eyebrows and tossed out words. Simply by altering her voice, the bard could make a casual remark as sharp as a missile or as persuasive as a caress: if Canola was irritating, she was also irresistible.

Bridey soon learnt that though Canola was clever with words, she was as clumsy and incompetent at things Bridey had been able to do since she could walk. Canola's hands were good for playing the harp and writing neatly with a quill, but she could not milk a cow, or handle a scythe, and she got in such a tangle with a basket that Bridey had to undo it all and start again. She was not able to bake, or row, or even use a knife, and Bridey wondered how she would survive if she did not have people to do such things for her. "Oh, we have servants for that," Canola said, and Bridey would stare, then flush with anger and storm away in disgust.

But Canola showed her how to whistle, and taught her comical rhymes and tongue-twisters. She let her ride Ceibhf-hionn whenever Bridey wanted, and even allowed her to coax a few anxious notes from her harp. It was this generosity that attracted Bridey and made her forget all the times her feelings were hurt.

Canola too was busy most of the day, with long difficult poems to learn, alphabets and secret ciphers to remember. The apprenticeship of a bard was long and gruelling: philosophy, music, mathematics, history, science . . . It seemed there was nothing that Canola could leave unlearned, and she sighed as she sat and listened to Eodain's boring voice patiently explaining yet another complex series of words, each of which

had several entirely different meanings. She fixed her eyes
on her teacher's long nose and her thoughts drifted to the
settlement across the marshes, where Bridey would be
working, weaving or milking the cow, or perhaps she had
borrowed Eadha's coracle and managed to escape over the
lake. Canola sighed again, wishing she could get away. The
class broke up and the young poets drifted towards the
refectory, joking and practising their satire on one another.
It was always competitive and seldom good-natured, and
Canola grew tired of the endless sarcasm and wit. She found
herself longing more and more for the straightforward conversation of her new friend.

"You're mixing with some odd people nowadays," remarked
one of the apprentices slyly. He wrinkled his nose and sniffed,
looking pained, and Canola walked off trembling.

"Oh, they drive me to distraction," she complained later as
she and Bridey took shelter from the rain in a tumbledown
stable.

"But how can you say that?" asked Bridey. "At least they're
interesting, not b-boring like . . ." She waved her hand vaguely
at the settlement which could be seen faintly through the
driving rain.

"Goodness, Bridey, you don't have to listen to them all day
long. And so vain . . .!" She tossed her head and uttered a few
caustic words. Bridey grinned, thinking that Canola was hardly
modest herself.

"But they're better than farmers and p-pig-boys," she said.

"No, they're not. They're just full of fancy notions and
scared of getting muck on their hands."

"Do you think farmers are better than poets?"

"Not better, just . . . more useful."

Bridey was amazed.

"Isn't poetry useful?"

"Oh, yes," Canola said. "Without poetry a person would
wither to nothing within a week." She shrugged. "I don't
know. No need to become an inflated prig just because you
know a few riddles."

Bridey glanced at Canola's earrings, her belt-buckle and her tartan breeches. She sniffed.

"I w-wish I was clever," she said.

"Oh, a poet is fed cleverness with a spoon from the cradle upwards."

"What do you mean?"

"Well, is it really clever to juggle words when you've been taught from the start? Besides, your baskets are clever."

"Huh!" Bridey looked at her hands and picked at the callouses.

They fell silent. Each knew that cleverness was not the whole story. Canola's parents could afford the twenty *sets* a year that a bard's apprenticeship cost. Bridey's mother could not afford the price of a thatcher to mend the roof, so she patched it with wicker and put down buckets when it rained. Canola was not especially clever: she was lucky.

Bridey narrowed her eyes thoughtfully.

"I suppose that cleverness is . . . well, finding something out *before* anyone tells you. Learning on your own," she shrugged, "I don't know."

Canola nodded.

"Do you know," she said, "the most beautiful words I ever heard in my life were spoken by a woman who could not speak at all."

"How?" Bridey waited, but Canola only smiled.

"Listen . . ." she said, and put a finger to her lips.

There was silence.

The next day the sun shone again and they were walking in the woods. Bridey was contented, all her irritability and crossness had vanished, and she had not visited the crown hidden below the willows for almost a week. But it was still there at the back of her mind, like an unsprung trap.

Canola was looking up into the branches of a beech tree.

"If you weren't a weaver," she asked, "what would you be?"

Bridey followed Canola's gaze and saw, in the maze of leaves, a fat thrush watching them with a round eye. She did not have to think for long.

"I'd be a man," she said distinctly, "and ride a tall white horse with black points, and have a long sword and cloak lined with ermine, and a goshawk with silver jesses ..." She flung out her arm to send her hawk up into the sky.

"By the Cross of the Carpenter!" swore Canola. "Why a man? Goodness, have you lost your mind?" And she wiped her eyes, unable to hide her amusement. "And what would you do then – gallop about chopping people to bits?"

Bridey waited for her to be quiet.

"I would f-fight for freedom," she said solemnly, and Canola stopped laughing.

"A noble sentiment," she remarked drily. "And whose freedom would that be exactly?"

Bridey was confused and fell silent. She remembered the crown in its hiding place and suddenly she hated the secret that was like a shadow spoiling her happiness.

"I've got something to show you," she said.

They took the boat without asking Eadha. With both girls in the little coracle it floated dangerously low in the water, and Bridey told Canola to keep still. "It'll go over, otherwise," she said, "and we'll have to swim." But Canola seemed quite happy with the suggestion and continued to bob up and down until the boat lurched and water splashed over the side, wetting their feet. Bridey did not laugh; she was becoming nervous.

"So, what is this mystery?" inquired Canola, narrowing her eyes.

"Wait and see," said Bridey, and she concentrated on rowing.

When they got to the willows, Bridey was sweating. She had changed her mind and was wondering why she had invited this sharp-tongued poet to share her treasure. Her crown was the only thing that made her special, and she did not want to share it.

"Come on, then," said Canola brightly, "let me have a look."

Unwillingly, Bridey leaned down and searched among the

roots for the floury sack that contained the crown. She wanted
to keep it a secret, and yet something made her draw it out and
lay it on the bank. The sack fell away and there, on the grass,
was the crown.

Canola said nothing. For a minute she stared at the ring of
yellow metal where it rested, dull and dented, then she said,
"Well, you're half-way to becoming a warrior queen already,
with a crown like this. Wherever did you find it?"

"It wasn't me," said Bridey. "It was Eadha – down among
the reeds in the m-marshes. I made him give it to me. It was
not . . . for him."

"No, indeed," agreed Canola, "not safe for a boy. But I
wonder . . ." She fell silent.

Bridey put out her hands and picked up the old crown.
Tilting her neck slightly, she placed it on her head, then she
looked at Canola.

"By St. Brigit," said the poet, "it suits you," and she gazed at
Bridey, her eyes wide with admiration. But she was also a little
shocked, for Bridey's face had changed. She seemed older, and
there was something menacing in her green eyes that made
Canola shiver. As she looked at Bridey she felt again that
strange sensation, as if she looked into a mirror and saw another
facet of herself – the same, yet not so. A passage of her
Midsummer poem came into her mind:

> *". . . The same bright flame that heats the forge*
> *Is raging in my pitiless heart;*
> *The band of spiralled gold I'll find –*
> *Or wrench this miserable world apart . . ."*

Her voice wavered, but her eyes were fixed steady on the slim
circle of gold on Bridey's head.

"So you – you think it's . . ." Bridey said, and with trembling
fingers she took the crown from her head and laid it back on the
grass. "Could it really belong to . . .?"

The air thrummed with heat. There was no sound but the
distant bird-song and the slow lapping of the lake. When
Canola spoke her voice was loud and embarrassed.

"When you put it on I – I felt as if I was looking at myself; it was very strange. I don't understand at all, but it's as if, for a moment, we were the same person. It's nonsense, of course ..." and she pushed the damp hair from her forehead, then recited:

"... I face the east, and spill a tide
Of blood across an eager land.
I face the west, and silver harps
Whisper beneath the poet's hand ..."

She sat back and looked hard at Bridey.

"Do you see," she said, "the two faces of Brigit: poet and ..."

"Warrior!" exclaimed Bridey, suddenly frightened. "But I'm not a warrior!"

"Remember what you said," replied Canola slowly. "A long sword and a cloak lined with ermine."

"That's a daydream," Bridey replied sharply, but as she spoke she remembered the blood on her hands and the thrill as her sword slashed down, and the screams of the people who ran before her ...

"*NO-O!*" she cried out in pain.

"Bridey, Bridey, what is it?" Canola gripped Bridey by the shoulders and leaned forward to comfort her. She was scared.

"I don't want to ... I don't *want* to," Bridey moaned, swaying back and forth. "I only wanted to ride a tall horse. I didn't want all this blood. Oh, if only I could make it go away!" and she started to strike herself with her fists, beating at her temples where the golden crown had so recently rested.

"*Stop!*" cried Canola, horrified. "Don't, please!" and she put her arms round the desperate girl, rocking her gently to and fro, stroking her face and murmuring softly, "There, it's all right ... quiet, now."

Within a few minutes Bridey was calm, and she leaned against Canola ashamed and confused. It seemed as if her mind was not her own, ideas and savage thoughts had claimed it for their battleground.

"What's happening?" she asked weakly. "Do you know?"

"No," Canola shook her head. Beside her flax-coloured plaits, Bridey's hair was as black as a raven's. "No, I don't understand at all. But perhaps I can ask Liadan."

"No!" Bridey sat up. "No, you mustn't tell anyone."

"Why not?"

Bridey was silent. She did not know why she should object so strongly, but she knew she wanted this thing to remain a secret between the two of them. "Please don't tell," she said, "not yet. Not till we understand."

Canola nodded but looked dubious. She touched the crown, tracing its spirals with her fingers, then pulled the sack over it.

"Put it back," she said.

Sorcha was waiting when they got back to the settlement.

"Where have you been?" she cried in exasperation. "I've been looking everywhere. Mother wants you, Bridey. And you," she frowned at Canola, "are wanted at the convent."

The girls sighed and glanced at each other with resignation.

"Tomorrow?" whispered Canola, and Bridey nodded.

But the next day Bridey was kept at home all day with Eadha, weeding the field behind the house and mending a pile of baskets left by the miller. The day after that, when she ran to find Canola, she was surprised to find the convent clearing busy with horses and people, and as she searched the crowd she saw Ceibhfhionn, Canola's skewbald pony.

"Canola! What's happening?"

The young poet looked up from tightening Ceibhfhionn's girth. She looked angry.

"Oh, it's you. I wondered if you'd turn up." She spat out the words as her fingers fought with the stubborn straps.

"What do you mean? What's g-going on?"

"What does it look like? We're leaving." Canola turned and glowered behind her at the other poets. She was furious with Bridey and unable to look at her. "Where were you yesterday?"

"I c-couldn't get away," she protested. "It wasn't my f-fault."

"Oh, w-wasn't it? Well, it's t-too late now!"

Bridey's eyes smarted. She wanted to hit Canola for mocking her, but the poet wouldn't stop talking.

". . . then three harp-strings broke and everyone laughed, and I got into trouble with Eodain because I don't know my verses; and she's told Liadan, so she's angry too and . . . I hate them!" She tugged furiously at the girth and buried her face in Ceibhfhionn's flank.

Bridey looked at the ground. All the happiness she had felt in the last week disappeared and was replaced by a cold, hard feeling. She clamped her teeth onto her bottom lip to stop it trembling.

"B-but . . ." she said, and was unable to continue.

Canola swore.

"It's not fair. They drag us about, never letting us stay anywhere, never letting us do anything. 'Don't be friendly with the farmers,' they say. 'They're not our sort.' Well, it's stupid and I'm sick of it," and she lifted her eyes defiantly. "I'll leave them one day, I will!" But even as she spoke both girls saw the careful eyes of Liadan and the Abbess watching them from the door of the sanctuary. Canola whispered savagely, "I've had enough of poetry. I'll get away from them, I swear it."

Bridey opened her mouth long enough to say, "D-don't be silly! Anyway, you can't do anything about it. None of us can do anything about it. It's just the way things are. I-I . . ." but her voice cracked and she fell silent, knowing their last minutes together were being wasted. The bards were mounting up and the Abbess was making a pretty speech of farewell. Liadan was replying wittily, and the polite laughter of the convent women filled the clearing. Canola swung up into the saddle.

"You c-can't go!" Bridey blurted, looking up. Canola's anger vanished and she suddenly looked lost.

"Watch the woods, Bridey," she said in a different voice. "I'll get back, somehow."

Bridey nodded but could not speak. The procession moved

off through the oaks accompanied by the delicate sound of bells, and Bridey stumbled back beneath the cover of the trees. Without looking back, she started to run through the woods in the direction of the marshes.

part two

8. the king's madness

I am fair among the flowers ...

Summer passed and it seemed to Bridey that her world had
shrunk in size; nothing in it interested her any more and she
hated everything she did. From the time she got up to the time
she went to bed there was nothing but work, work that tore her
hands and hurt her back, making her legs cramp and her feet
ache. She seldom spoke and when she did her tongue was
clumsy from lack of use, and she knew that anyone who
listened would see what an ugly fool she had become. At the
end of every month her depression increased and she would lie
brooding on her cot in the smoky hut, savouring the bleak
feeling inside her.

"What's the matter, Bridey?" Eadha would ask, nervously
putting out a hand to touch her, his face solemn with worry.
"Why are you unhappy?" But Bridey never answered and
merely turned over and stared at the flaking clay wall, feeling
her body heavy and lifeless on the straw mattress.

Sometimes her mother stood over her, despairing at her
daughter. "For goodness' sake, Bridey! What's happening to
you? Where's all your life gone?" Her heart ached for the girl,
but she had enough to worry about with a leaking roof, a dry
cow and mounting debts. At times she cursed her daughters.
She seemed to have spent all her life taking care of people but
no one took care of her. What had happened to Bridey? Who
was this heavy-limbed creature with bloodshot eyes and a
wicked tongue? She had been such a happy baby . . . little baby
Brigit . . .

Her mother's attention only increased Bridey's frustration,

and she would fling herself out of the house, her hands itching to pull the bowls from the shelves and shatter them on the floor, wanting to yell and scream and break the door down.

There had never been a harder harvest. The sun shone ceaselessly from the sky with no breath of wind from across the lake to give relief. Midges swarmed above the marshes and the bog-water gleamed, inviting children to stray among the tussocks and drown. The women worked mindlessly, like their animals. With the men away there were half as many hands to do the work. Not a cloud passed across the face of the sun.

Occasionally a messenger galloped through bringing news of the war, speaking in brave, flowery words. But the news was always the same: Breagh of the New Hand led his men from one defeat to the next; the land was in chaos, and every man of Connacht was needed to help turn the tide. Victory, of course, was certain. The last men went away and soon the settlement seemed scarcely to be breathing. Then came reports of scavenging mercenaries who roamed the woods and plains ransacking and burning every farm or convent they passed, and the women sharpened their kitchen knives. But they did not speak of their fear, and their homes had never seemed so quiet before.

Whenever possible – at first light, or in the cool of the evening when the exhausted harvesters had thrown down their scythes and gone home – Bridey dragged herself into the woods. In the shade of the oak groves her spirits lifted slightly, and she would look down the little tracks as she walked, alert for any sound of travellers. But not a soul passed through the forest these days. The settlement was alone, surrounded by marshes and trees.

She had moved the golden crown from its hiding place beneath the willows to a new place deep in the cleft of a dying beech. Whenever she came to the woods she pulled it out and stared at the spirals, as if they would help her make sense of her miserable lethargy.

Three months had passed since the court of Liadan had left the convent clearing, bound for their next destination. Now the weather was cold, the harvest was over and every barn was filled to the roof with grain and fodder. Strings of onions hung from the rafters, and outhouses were fragrant with vegetables. Deep in the woods the pigs grunted, feasting on nuts as they unwittingly fattened themselves for winter. It was Gort, the month of Ivy, the leaves were brown on the trees, and underfoot was a carpet of gold. Bridey, walking through the woods, smelled autumn in the air and saw the ivy spiralling up and up, the only greenery left. She had never dreaded the winter as much as she did this year, and despite the beauty of the woods it seemed as if there was death in every breath she took.

One day towards the end of the month she slipped away from home, from her mother and Sorcha who were busy weaving huge squares for the repair of some broken-down sheep-pens. They did not see her go, and Eadha, who followed her for a few yards, was soon angrily dismissed.

"Go home, boy," she hissed. "Can't you ever leave me in peace?"

Eadha looked hurt, then angry.

"Oh, fall in the bog, you witch," he spat, and turned away, his eyes stinging. He missed Bridey and couldn't understand why she was so changed. He knew she was unhappy but didn't know why this should make her cruel. She never wanted to play any more, or tell him stories. She was no fun, just grown-up and stupid.

Bridey was cruel. Watching the hurt on the boy's face she felt a brief spurt of pleasure, and wanting to hurt him further she put out a hand and shoved him down in a patch of mud. She bit her lip and walked away, leaving him wailing.

Yet again, as if visiting a grave, she went to the place where she had last seen Canola, and soon her mind was full of the young poet: good memories of the way they had laughed; bitter, jealous recollections of the girl's wit and confidence. It was a muddle and Bridey could not untangle it. She knew Canola would not come, but every day she came to the woods to watch for her return. When she asked the Abbess, Fionnuala said, "Oh no, they won't be back this year. They'll be in

77

Corkaguiney by now ... or were they going further north? I can't remember," and Bridey sighed and wandered off, unable to keep away from the woods, where she sat and watched the endlessly falling leaves.

Today it was grey and misty with a bitter wind blowing over the marshes, and Bridey pulled her woollen cloak close about her shoulders. Nearing the convent clearing she saw the stone of St. Brigit which stood near the sanctuary. The carved face of the saint was blank and patient. A few sheep cropped the turf, their matted fleece tugged by the wind, and they looked up as Bridey came near, gazing at her with the same blank expression as the statue, before turning and running off, tails bouncing.

Nothing was astir in the convent and the only sign of life was a thin ribbon of smoke rising from the refectory. Bridey turned away and began to walk into the woods, keeping off the path for fear of being seen. Deeper she went until she came to a place where a small stream crossed the path, then she fetched the old crown from the beech tree and sat down to watch the water as it tumbled round the stepping stones.

Time passed and Bridey sat so still that a squirrel gathering nuts came closer, rustling among the leaves in search of acorns. Bridey opened her eyes and watched absent-mindedly. The squirrel stopped and sat up. Dropping its acorn, it sprang up a nearby tree: it had heard something. Bridey, resting her head on her knees, leaned forward to listen, but the only sound was the wind in the branches.

Then she heard voices.

She jerked her head up and looked around. She could see nothing, but getting up she darted behind a tree, her cloak a swirl of russet. Horsemen were approaching and the sound of the horses' feet in the leaves was like a slow sighing. Bridey stared, her cheek pressed against the trunk.

It was a pathetic sight.

The riders did not trot past with chiming harness, or hold up their heads, proud and defiant, with smooth, sleek hair. They had bridles made of rope and they rode with their heads bowed, in silence. Bridey stared at the dismal limping ponies and the filthy men who rode them. As they drew nearer she recognised them and began to tremble.

Gegra the Shepherd came first, his tattered legs kicking the belly of his pony with mindless, rhythmic thumps. His head was bound in a dirty cloth and his left eye was a closed purple slit in his face. His right eye stared fixedly between the pony's drooping ears as he swiped at its neck with a stick.

Next came Dian, his brother, older than Gegra. He had been a man unaccustomed to company, other than that of the bedraggled sheep he tended on the plains. Now he could barely sit astride his horse and he lolled from side to side, his bony knuckles clenched in the horse's mane. One leg hung uselessly and his trousers were dark and stiff with blood.

Behind Dian, stumbling in the leaves and leading a pony whose hollow coughing showed it near collapse, came Bres the swineherd.

"Come on, you filthy brute, can't you smell your stable?" he muttered, pulling viciously at the pony's mouth, but the animal only stumbled and coughed, then gave a long, exhausted shudder. "That's if your stable still stands," and he wiped his nose on his sleeve and pulled again at the reins.

Cormac, who brought up the rear, drew a deep breath, trying to stifle his tears. Clumsily he wiped his face with the back of his hand, cleared his throat, then fumbled for the reins, but they had fallen down and now hung out of reach between his pony's ears. His face crumpled and his sobs grew louder. His right arm had been severed at the shoulder and where it had been was nothing but a bulge of cloth, black with dirt and blood. Unable to balance properly, he swayed uncertainly, but could not reach the reins. The pony's feet soon became entangled and Cormac wept helplessly, his good hand clawing at his face as he swayed and lurched in the saddle.

"Pull yourself together, you whining idiot," jeered Bres, as he stopped to untangle the reins. "Keep hold and keep your mouth shut!" He hated Cormac for his pain and helplessness; hated the new lopsidedness and found it sickening. He knew he should be kind, but he couldn't help himself. Why did Cormac have to snivel and whine?

"Leave him alone, Bres," called Gegra harshly. "He's not the only one who's crying. And he's lost more than you."

Bres ground his teeth. He had not shed a tear since he had covered his father's mangled body with a thin layer of dirt and leaves. He vowed that he would never weep again. He dreaded his own weakness.

"How shall I tell them at home?" he asked. "We said we'd bring back jewels and gold and a Taran head in a sack ..." What he had thought would be a series of elegant battles had turned out to be no more than a weary slog from one mad rout to the next. He almost wished he had fallen beside his father, and yet he clung savagely to life.

"And all that brave talk at the start," said Gegra bitterly, "before we knew the strength of their armies ... or the stupidity of our King."

"It wasn't the King," said Dian, raising his head and gazing blearily about him. "He was ill-advised. It was that pretty Prince Lir, that milk-fed foundling. He has bewitched the King, they say, and fills his ears with deadly mischief."

"You're a fool," said Gegra coldly. "We were bought cheap, and it was our own blindness that pulled us along."

"You are disloyal," said Dian, "and you were always a coward, but *your* so-called blindness has only lost you an eye. Others have fared worse."

Gegra shrugged.

Bridey, watching from her hiding place, remembered these men as they had been when they had ridden away in what seemed now like another life. Then, they had been full of joy and adventure: it would be like in the poems – a pageant of bright colours and brave men ... They would love each other and share everything – food, dreams, fears ... Now half of them were dead and those that remained were set against each other.

She saw Gegra fumble in his pocket. For a moment he held something in his hand, staring at it with a look of intense bitterness; then, with an oath, he threw it from him. It landed a foot away from Bridey and silently she put out a cold hand to pick it up. It was the gold coin that had helped lure Gegra away. She examined it closely, disarmed by the rearing horse and the mysterious letters. How pretty it was! How Gegra's children would have marvelled at it . . . The touch of the treacherous gold made her dizzy. Into her mind came a picture of a settlement like her own, a farmstead surrounded by marsh. She smelled fire as the huts burned, and heard the screaming of children trapped inside . . . Taran children, enemy children murdered by Gegra . . .

There was silence as the men passed slowly by, Gegra weeping from his one good eye. Bridey trembled. This was it. This was the result of all her savage imaginings. An evil tide was loose and this was the result, all this dirt and blood. Her mouth tasted foul and she spat repeatedly onto the ground, shivering violently. The four wounded riders were almost out of sight, and with an effort she pulled herself up and slowly began to follow them. Ducking behind trees and treading lightly, she managed to hear more of their muffled conversation.

". . . but who will tell them?" Bres was musing, half-aloud. When the others did not reply, he continued to speak to himself, his voice anxious and fretful. "Why does it have to be me? I can't tell them . . . So many dead after all, where will I start? With Miach and Feargal and Donagha? Or with our foolhardy wheelwright and that crawling brute Conall? All dead, picked by crows and covered in flies. And no one knows where the rest went. Perhaps they're still wandering about in the bogs of Midhe, starving to death because our King burned the harvest. By St. Brigit it was a bad day when Breagh came to the throne. Ha!" He spat contemptuously on the ground. "I would've killed him myself, but I know there's no more to a dead man than a bit of meat and gristle. If the soul goes anywhere it's into the stomach of a raven."

"You blasphemous fool!" wheezed Dian, struggling for breath, his thin face twisted with rage and his hands, clamped in the pony's mane, trembling with passion. "Our dead are rejoicing now in Paradise. Why does the sun set, if not to light the Blessed Isles?"

Gegra, overhearing, laughed nastily.

"Brother, you sound like one of these new prating preachers. Well, don't ask me to believe in an eastern carpenter and a crowd of chanting monks."

Dian was silent. The woods were quiet, except for the steady cough of Bres's horse.

Coming in sight of the low buildings and the beehive cells scattered in the little clearing, the men drew rein. For a second they watched the thin line of smoke and the ragged sheep grazing about the stone of St. Brigit. Then Gegra's pony, smelling perhaps the wood-smoke and the convent stables, broke into a shambling trot.

Cormac uttered a wild cry, but his pony would go no faster.

"Oh, Brigit! Thank you!" called the young man. "Thank you, merciful mother and maiden, Queen of Heaven . . ."

Bridey shivered at the sound of his voice. If the dead could speak they would sound like this. She stared as the four riders came to a halt in the centre of the convent clearing. She heard the startled shouts of the women as they ran from their cells, and their dismay when they saw who the travellers were. She saw the Abbess run forward to help Cormac from the saddle, and heard her voice, sharp and frightened. Then a noise from behind made her turn and duck behind a bush. Here came another rider, this time at a canter, and Bridey imagined a merciless captain who would take the head from her shoulders and not even stop to look. The rider pulled up a few yards from her.

"Bridey! Is that you? Are you deaf? I thought you'd never turn round. What are you doing behind that bush?"

It was Canola, looking just the same with her pale hair loose about her face, leaping from the saddle, running over to Bridey and dragging her out of the undergrowth.

"Goodness, what a journey!" she said. "The whole of Erin's in a turmoil. We have to do something about this madness, you know, or there'll be no one left at all."

9. the Riddle

I am the oak and the lightning that blasts it . . .

Canola came from an old and noble family in the far north of Erin, but she remembered little about them, because when she was nine her parents had sent her to Liadan of Corkaguiney to be given a full education and the opportunity of reaching the honoured position of bard. It was an expensive business, but they were wealthy people, and the girl showed such promise that it seemed a pity to keep her at home where her gifts would remain undeveloped. Her elder brothers had already been sent from home to live in a household closer to the King's court.

Ever since she could talk Canola had been clever with words, and her fingers had proved skilful with the harp. She was an odd child, with her quick tongue and strange colourless hair, given to fits of crying and periods of unhappy withdrawal. Her parents were unnerved by their youngest child: the discipline of Liadan's court would be good for her.

Canola left home with nothing but a change of clothes and one or two treasured possessions that she carried in a leather pouch. She had never liked toys, preferring to make her games from the things she saw about her. But her mother had once carved a doll for her daughter from a piece of wood, and when Canola went to Liadan she took little that could give her comfort, apart from the doll that she held close during the night.

Her mother had not stopped her from being sent away, and Canola hated her. On the dreadful morning when she had been pushed into the saddle behind strange thin Eodain who had come to take her away for the long apprenticeship, her mother

83

had given Canola a package bound in a gold embroidered cloth. "Take this, child," she had said, "it is for you, handed down by my grandmother to me. When you can read you'll be able to understand it ... for I've no idea what it means," and the woman had turned away, reluctant to meet her daughter's eyes.

Canola had listened, convinced her mother could not love her if she was sending her away. She looked past her to where her father stood stiffly nearby, dressed in jewels and fur, and saw him raise his hand to wave. She did not wave back. She refused to be brave.

In the years that followed she saw them only occasionally, at official functions, and their meetings were embarrassed and formal. They were like strangers. Her brothers she had never seen again, and she tried to forget about them. Slowly she forgot her home in the north and adapted to her new life.

But the loneliness stayed with her. She learned to hide it behind a stream of words as she became sharp and clever. At first she was bullied, the children pulled her pale plaits and called her a 'yellow-hair'. But then they grew to like her and she to like them, but coolly, and without passion. She was fond of Eodain, her teacher, and she revered Liadan – but if ever Canola started to love with too great a warmth, she would pull back, remembering the day she had been sent away.

When she rode into the Abbess Fionnuala's clearing and saw Bridey's face – so angry and so similar to her own – she had felt a curiosity that quite surprised her. She had to get to know this sullen farm-girl, whether Bridey wanted it or not, and as their friendship developed Canola found it hard to maintain her usual reserve. Bridey was unlike anyone she had ever met. She was not smooth-tongued or brilliant like the poets, but thoughtful and deliberate in her speech, quick and clumsy in her anger. Canola often wanted to tease her for her unpolished ways; it was customary for the poets to despise those less lucky than themselves, and at times Canola did despise Bridey. She was trained to see farmers as less important: above the animals, but far below the poets, and Canola found it hard to go against this training. Yet she also admired the young basket-weaver, and even envied her. Bridey had a real home, sisters and a brother, things that Canola could never have. She found herself wanting to change places.

When Liadan called her court together and told them to prepare for departure, Canola was devastated. She hated Liadan for making her leave, hated Eodain for trying to be kind. It was the same angry emptiness she felt when she thought of her mother, as if some part of her had been severed. How had she been so careless? This was what happened when you made friends. She almost hated Bridey because she had come to love her.

In the month that followed, as the court travelled slowly through the hot countryside, Canola often thought of her, remembering the girl's calloused hands and reluctant smile, and the generous laughter that Canola's words had brought forth. Most of all, in the evenings spent round the fires, listening to the songs and ballads, Canola pictured Bridey the day she had worn the crown, remembering the friendly face that had become pitiless and beautiful, and she felt a stab of jealousy that this face, so like her own, could be so hard and lovely. When Bridey had laid the crown back on the grass, she once more became Bridey – reliable and unqueenly – and Canola had been reassured. But she had never forgotten the change that had taken place – like looking in a mirror and seeing someone else.

In the autumn, Liadan had been summoned to Cruachan by the King, and Canola had returned with Eodain and the younger apprentices to Corkaguiney, to spend the winter deep in study. On the borders of Connacht the war raged fiercely, and Canola often feared for Bridey, far away in the unprotected lakeside settlement.

The nights were growing colder and the leaves on the trees starting to lose their green, when Eodain had called her students to her to give them a solemn lecture on the new course of study they were about to embark upon. With many long words she explained that they were now ready to learn one of the sacred *oghams*, one of the most ancient alphabets of all, and the most secret. "You will be able to talk to the birds," she said, as her hands moved gracefully in the secret signs and her long nose quivered. "Once you have conquered the Beth-Luis-Nion, the very trees will vie for your conversation."

For the following two weeks they had struggled to grasp the rudiments of this complex alphabet, not simply the way to write it, but the corresponding sign to make with the hand, the corresponding tree, colour and bird, and the many layers of meaning attached to each cipher. Within the first few days Canola realised that this new knowledge was to be more useful to her than even Eodain had suspected. Alone in her *clocháin*, she studied with more concentration than ever before.

Three years before, on her tenth birthday, Canola had been ceremoniously presented – by Liadan herself – with her very own cell on the outskirts of the rambling collection of huts and buildings that was Corkaguiney. This little mound of mud and wattle, with its chimney and tiny window, and a coffer for books at the end of the narrow bed, was home to the young poet, and she loved it. It was a place both private and quiet, where she spent long hours while the other apprentices gathered in the meeting-house. Now, armed with her new insight, she retreated there, and in the bottom of the wooden coffer she found the gift, wrapped in embroidered fabric, that her mother had given her so many years ago.

Unfolding the finely-stitched cloth, Canola ran her hands over the smooth wooden block. It was of beech and so old that the wood was almost black. The corners were chipped and rounded with much handling, and the ancient characters carved on its surface gleamed in the dim light of the cell.

How many times since being sent away had Canola taken out the beech block and looked at it, feeling a link to the mother she had left behind? She loved the feel of the wood and had often tried in vain to understand the words. With her fingers she traced the whirls and spirals carved on the border, but the meaning of the block had been hidden. Now, learning the Beth-Luis-Nion, she had begun to be able to read the words. She told no one, but at last after long weeks of exhaustive work, Canola could read most of the ciphers inscribed on the block.

She could read the words, but their meaning was too obscure, and she rocked slowly to and fro on the bed, whispering the mysterious lines over and over, " . . . then Warrior and Poet gladly meet . . . " This part of the riddle at least was clear: it was about Brigit. Alone at night she watched the flickering flame of her candle and wondered what to do.

One night when the wind was howling about the cell and the creaking of the branches in the trees was loud and ominous, Canola fell asleep and dreamed that she was standing in the convent clearing of Abbess Fionnuala. It was completely deserted – even the sheep had fled. Only the stone of St. Brigit stood, casting a long shadow across the cropped turf. Canola looked at the carved features. The eyes were no longer blank; they were alive, calling her. *Riddler, poet and peace-maker . . .* came the imaginary voice . . . *I need you . . . I need you to find . . .*

She awoke sweating, her heart pounding, and knew she must leave. She was no coward, but the thought of travelling alone for fifty miles filled her with fear. Connacht was no longer safe for travellers, of that she was certain, for bands of soldiers roamed the plains. Although no one knew if they were of Connacht or of Tara, it made no difference, for they burned and murdered where they passed. She lay awake. She knew the roads and had a good knowledge of the stars, but still she was sure she would get lost. She must be mad – a girl on her own, not even a full bard – to think of such a journey. Then she remembered the old songs, songs of heroines of ancient days, who had risked their lives in pursuit of a noble end. "This will be my quest," she whispered, watching the candle-flame dip and sway and the shadows shifting on the walls. She did not know what she was to do when she got there, but she could not ignore Brigit's call. She must go back to the marsh settlement.

She must find Bridey.

Before dawn she slipped across to the kitchens and stole two wineskins and a couple of large bannocks from the bread-basket by the door. She filled one wineskin with water from the well, and another with mead from the cask outside the refectory. Light was beginning to filter across the sky as she tiptoed over the frosty grass towards the stable. Her stomach fluttered with anticipation, and the sight of her breath clouding the air in the deserted courtyard gave her a thrill of pleasure. She felt brave and important, and was surprised how careful and quiet she was able to be, considering the level of her excitement. This morning, as she made her preparations, Canola felt she was capable of anything.

Putting the wineskins, the beech tablet and the bread deep into the saddlebags, she led Ceibhfhionn from the stable. The pony's hooves on the stones rang out in the cold air, and Canola was sure that at any moment someone would run out and discover her. She forced herself to be calm as she led Ceibhfhionn slowly over the crisp grass towards the gates. Looping the reins over her wrist she put her shoulder to the heavy bar and pushed. With a groan the gates swung open and the pony plodded through. Before Canola shut the doors she stopped and laid a small piece of parchment on the ground just inside. She had taken this from her precious store of writing materials in her coffer, and last night inscribed, in the Beth-Luis-Nion, these words:

"Please do not follow. I go because I have to," and beneath the message she had drawn a harp, the symbol of Canola.

Outside the gates the world was beginning to wake. Birds called from the trees and a deep mist hung over the river. Soon people would be getting up. She had no time to lose.

All at once she was assailed by doubts. She must be a fool to think she could get away with it. Eodain would send someone to fetch her back, or she would get murdered on the road by mercenaries. Even if she ever reached the marshlands, how was she to know that Bridey would be glad to see her? Suddenly Canola was convinced she would be turned away. Bridey did not really like her, she hated her for her learning and her soft hands. Canola frowned. The thought of Bridey decided her. "I don't care what you think," she muttered angrily, and swinging herself into the saddle, she nudged Ceibhfhionn forward with her heels. It was too late now, she could not stay. Once over the wooden bridge that crossed the wide river, Canola gave the pony a kick and Ceibhfhionn broke into a canter. Soon they were upon the broad path that led to the north.

Five days later Canola reached the oak woods surrounding the convent of St. Brigit, and there, crouching behind a bush in her russet cloak, was Bridey, staring at her as if she was a ghost.

Canola could not stop grinning, however hard she tried, and her teeth were chattering with nerves.

"Well, Bridey?"

"Canola!"

"The very same."

"You look d-different."

"So do you."

"Oh, I'm the s-same."

But Canola was shocked by Bridey's appearance. When she had last seen her she had been brown from the sun – angry-looking, but healthy. Now there were dark rings round her eyes and her skin was pale. Without thinking, Canola put out a hand and traced the shadows in her cheeks. Her action took them both by surprise, and Bridey reacted awkwardly:

"You don't look s-so good yourself. You're filthy."

Days of travelling through rough country, of being hungry and frightened and tired, had left Canola wild and dirty, not at all the well-groomed poet that Bridey had watched ride away. Her cloak was torn and her tartan breeches were caked in mud.

"Are you surprised?" exclaimed Canola. "All the way from Corkaguiney and I got lost twice somewhere over there," and she waved vaguely in the direction of the lake.

Silence fell and they could think of nothing else to say. They had waited so long for this. Bridey began to walk further into the woods, picking her way along a narrow path that was little used by the people from the settlement. Canola followed, leading Ceibhfhionn. At last Bridey said falteringly, "I thought I'd go m-mad. I felt like a f-fox in a trap. If only I knew what to do, it wouldn't be so bad." She looked back down the path. "Did you see those men? And most of them are dead, they say, and all we do is weave more baskets and wait for the soldiers to come and chop us to bits." It was a relief to talk. She felt suddenly hopeful. Even with the memory of Cormac fresh in her mind it would be better with Canola here. She knew she would not be consumed by her own violent thoughts. Even if men came with swords to kill her, the dark conflict in her mind could no longer destroy her.

"But w-why are you here? How did you get away?" She clasped Canola's arm.

Canola pushed her hair off her forehead.

"Oh, getting away was the easy part. The rest wasn't so simple," and she began to tell Bridey about the journey north from Corkaguiney. There had been a river to cross, and marshes; some of the roads she did not recognise and some were overgrown. Twice she had lost herself and been forced to ask the way of people working in the fields. She had covered her hair and spoken in gruff monosyllables like a boy, knowing how suspicious they would be of a girl travelling alone. Once she had called to a man cutting peat. Something about the way he glanced at his friend and then jumped down from the carefully stacked turf blocks had made her stick her heels into Ceibhfhionn's sides and gallop off.

But the nights were worse, sleeping in damp hollows, hardly daring to breathe in case there were men nearby. One morning she woke to find that she had camped in what obviously had been the site of a bloody battle between soldiers. She had slept with her head pillowed in the soft earth of a newly dug grave.

" . . . and if ever heather blooms again on such a blood-soaked patch of bog, I'll be surprised. How is it the poets never sing of the smell of blood when it's been drying in the sun, or the stench of a body floating in bog-water?"

Bridey said dully, "I always thought f-fighting would be fun . . . " She stopped, remembering the wounded men. She had dreamed of riding into battle with a sharp sword, but now the reality of it sickened her.

Canola continued, "Ah, you've heard the bards singing of glory and brave deeds, and of how the young men grow into heroes, and how good and kindly they are. Well," she lowered her voice grimly, "I've sung those songs and I thought they were true. But when I saw the bodies lying twisted and stinking in the marshes with their eyes picked by crows . . . I don't think I'll be singing of brave deeds again." Her hands were trembling as she fumbled with the reins and patted Ceibhfhionn's smooth neck. "I have done with ballads, endless words . . . on and on . . ."

"B-but words don't always lie," said Bridey, "they can be used to tell the truth, as well. It depends on who's talking . . . and what they're saying."

Canola shrugged, but Bridey went on more confidently, thinking of Cormac's grotesque injuries and Gegra's ruined face. "That's what the songs should be about: people after the fighting, the miserable state of them . . . You should make up songs about that. You've done all that studying."

Canola looked at her blankly.

"But I don't know how," she said, "not any more."

Bridey was shocked. Canola's words and gestures were frantic and painful, not graceful like they used to be, but then neither of them was as happy or irresponsible as they had been in the summer. It was as if their minds were no longer their own . . . they were in someone's power.

They walked for a while without speaking, the rustle of their feet in the leaves the only sound. At length Canola sighed and said, "The High King of Tara has gathered a force of two thousand men. He's marching towards Connacht, and he has joined with the Kings of Midhe and Cashel. King Breagh doesn't stand a chance. He's been called to talk peace many times but he won't lay down his sword," she snorted. "They say he's mad, you know. I even heard his own men have tried to kill him. Can you imagine, to be so hated and still to be the King?" She shook her head, "You'd think he'd give up."

Bridey pursed her lips

"He doesn't sound mad to me," she said. "Quite ordinary, really. If he gives up now, it'll prove he was wrong. Then everyone will have died for no reason. He's got to keep on to the end, or he'll look weak." She could sympathise with the King's recklessness, thinking back to her own warrior day-dreams, she could picture the wild determination that would not allow him to stop the slaughter. " . . . and of course he enjoys it, too," she said quietly.

Canola looked at her in dismay.

"What do you mean?"

"He enjoys it," Bridey repeated, "he likes to kill. Can't you understand that?" and she looked at Canola with curiosity.

"No, I cannot," said Canola simply, and Bridey knew she would not be able to convey the ghastly thrill of exercising a savage power, of hunting down, of killing.

"I have d-dreams," she said, and remembering the weight of the golden crown on her temples, her voice sank to a whisper. "I h-hate them."

They walked on slowly. What Bridey said scared Canola and made her nervous, so she started talking too much – a stream of description – anything to keep Bridey from speaking. She told of the endless round of recitals and banquets she had attended, until King Breagh had summoned Liadan to his fortress at Cruachan. Liadan was powerful, but she could not refuse an order from the King, and leaving behind the younger poets, she had taken her court across the wide plain to the King's seat, where she had remained, attempting at every opportunity to take the deadly edge off his stupidity. "But though her satire is merciless," said Canola, "Breagh is such an idiot that she'll never be able to find a mark. And he doesn't have to heed her, after all. They say he's surrounded by druids who have sold out to the Tarans. And then there's this cousin of his, a spoilt Prince who Breagh's brought to the court for a whim. Some orphan he's taken a fancy to, some whelp sold to the King by parents who no longer bothered with him. They say he stinks of perfume and can barely wave his handkerchief because of the weight of his jewellery. Pah! What fools!" She kicked at the leaves, looking angry.

Bridey said nothing.

Soon they came to a place deep in the woods where two paths met and a pyramid of logs stood, covered in brambles and moss. They climbed to the top, sat down and listened to a thrush calling. Gradually Canola began to feel more cheerful. As she relaxed, the knot in her stomach that had developed over the last few days slowly began to ease. Remembering suddenly what it was that had brought her all the way to Bridey, she hopped off the logs and fetched the beech tablet in the embroidered cloth from Ceibhfhionn's saddlebag. Then she clambered back up and sat down close to Bridey, the package on her knees. Bridey did not say anything. Canola unwrapped the block and carefully folded the cloth. Briday leaned forward to look.

"What is it?" she asked slowly.

Canola considered. She did not really know what it was. It was her possession, it was from her mother, and she loved its dark wood and clumsy spirals. Recently it had become the focus of all her interest.

"It's a riddle, I think," she said, pointing at the patterns.

"Do you know what it says?"

"Some of it." She groaned. "Oh, you have no idea, Bridey! Four more alphabets since I last saw you, and endless verses ... I thought my head would burst! But at least it's been useful for a change. I never thought I'd be able to read this."

Bridey raised her eyebrows and stiffened. She did not even know one alphabet. It had not seemed to matter until now.

"I c-can't even spell my own name," she said.

Canola sighed. Here it was again. Bridey's ignorance embarrassed her; but it did not mean a lot, so why couldn't Bridey simply forget about it?

"Don't start that again, for goodness' sake. You know very well cleverness isn't in it."

"S-so you say."

They moved apart and there was an uncomfortable silence.

Canola was angry at Bridey for sulking, and Bridey was furious with Canola for knowing how to read. At last she said, "Just don't say it doesn't matter. It does. You know it."

"I'm sorry."

Bridey grunted and bent over the piece of wood. It was getting dark. The wood was smooth and cold.

"Look," she said suddenly, "spirals! Like the decorations on the crown. They're the same!"

"Well, this is probably as old. They're both from long ago. Oh, I wish I knew more."

Bridey looked thoughtful.

"The spirals are from the time of the Tuatha dé Danaan. Spirals were their magic."

"How do you know?"

"I'm not completely stupid," said Bridey coldly. "I do know a few things."

Canola bit her tongue. She had sounded smug and knowing, but she didn't feel it.

"Where did you find it?" continued Bridey, and as she glanced up she saw an expression of sullen anger flash across Canola's face. She put out a hand. "Where from?" she repeated.

"Oh, my mother gave it to me," Canola said airily. "I never knew why until a few weeks ago. 'You will know what I have given you when you are grown.' That's what she said."

Bridey was silent. She spent so much time wanting to get away from her family it was hard to sympathise with Canola for wanting a proper family herself. Life with Liadan must be so exciting compared to the drudgery of the settlement that she thought Canola was mad to complain. Then she remembered how resentful she had been when her own father died – her feelings of being left alone, of being deserted. Canola's feelings began to make more sense.

"I c-can be your family now . . . " she said tentatively, and was dismayed to see Canola's eyes fill with tears. "Oh, please don't," she blurted, "there isn't t-time."

Canola laughed and wiped her nose on her sleeve.

"Don't worry," she said. "I always cry when I think of my

94

mother. I'm quite used to it," and she took a deep breath and smiled bleakly.

Bridey bent back over the beech block.

"C-come on, then, if you're so clever – tell me what it says."

Canola shrugged.

"I haven't worked it all out yet. The difficult bit is at the end, and it's full of riddles I've never heard before. The first bit's easy," and she began to recite, using the voice Bridey had heard on Midsummer's night – soft and penetrating and slightly husky:

> *"When Aspen, born of Willow, wets his feet*
> *The golden spiral of the flame is lost,*
> *And cruel Brigit's anger burns so bright*
> *That steel is sharp and fire is burning hot;*
> *The Raven croaks, and death is all about . . .*

What's the matter?"

Bridey had stopped listening and was staring grumpily at the ground. Canola sighed. Why was it so difficult? What had she said wrong now?

"I can't do it on my own, you know, I need your help. Please, Bridey?"

"Go on, I'm listening."

> *" . . . until the wintry month of reeds is near.*
> *Then Brigit looks once more into her glass,*
> *And Warrior and Poet gladly meet*
> *To travel to the ancient Tomb of Reeds*
> *'Ere Samain Eve, or else the cause is lost . . . "*

She stopped.

"Is that all?" asked Bridey.

"No, but the rest is difficult. There's something about a . . . hermit, I think, and a shield. I'm not sure. And then something about losing what is found . . . but all that is too hard. The letters aren't all the same, and some of them have even been worn away, see?"

Bridey bent forward. The words had caused her hair to prickle at the back of her neck.

"When Aspen, born of Willow, wets his feet . . ." she repeated, "I think I've got that bit."

Canola waited.

"Well, Eadha's name means Aspen, and he's born of Willow because he's in our family – willow-weavers, you see." Her tone was matter of fact.

"But why should he wet his feet?"

"He's always getting soaked. I suppose it could be when he found the crown in the marshes, among the reeds."

"And that was the beginning of it all," mused Canola, " . . . when Brigit lost her crown and war broke out."

"But what about the rest?"

"Hmm . . . until the wintry month of reeds . . . Well, that's Ngetal, isn't it, which is in a few days' time. Then . . . Brigit looks once more into her glass . . . "

"And Warrior and Poet gladly meet," cried Bridey. "But that's us! It has to be." She jumped down from the log pile, waving her arms. "That's why I had the dreams: I found the crown and became the warrior." She shivered and looked sober. "And you're the poet, that's easy enough."

Canola had gone pale.

"But where do we find the Tomb of Reeds?"

" . . . before Samain Eve!"

The girls stared at each other in frustration.

"But that's only three days away." Canola jumped down too.

The birds had stopped singing and the woods were dark. Night had fallen without their noticing and a shuffling sound in the leaves nearby made them move together, startled. A pleasant voice inquired:

"I know I am in danger of intruding. Silly old men are always in danger of that. But if I may be so bold, is there, perhaps, some way in which I could be of assistance? A little translation of ancient runes, maybe? Or perhaps some early magic . . . "

Bridey and Canola stared, terrified.

Watching them with a shrewd expression on his lined face was Tahan the Greek.

10. the map

I am the queen of hives ...

Half an hour later they were standing outside Tahan's hut. An owl began to cry from a nearby treetop and deep within the hives the bees slept, silently guarding their queen.

Tahan moved about inside. "I am unused to visitors," he fussed. There was a rasp of flint and a light flared, throwing shadows across the clearing. The old man poked his head through the window.

"Come in, then, my young friends," he said, and pulled back his head. But his beard wound round the string of his drum and caught on a twig. He fumbled about, bleating softly.

Canola felt giggles welling up at the sight of the old man's efforts. She bit her lips and nudged Bridey, but saw she was scowling. She sighed and ran over to disentangle Tahan from his window.

"Kind of you, my dear," he said, smoothing the tangled beard and eyeing her intently. "What elegant manners artists have."

Canola blushed uneasily as he looked past her to where Bridey sulked in the shadows.

"Come, willow-woman, won't you join us? We have urgent business, and ..." He smiled toothlessly. Bridey came forward slowly. Of course, she thought, it would be Canola who managed to please the filthy old man. She followed the poet inside and pulled shut the door. They stood back as the old man bustled about. There was so little room that they had to stand close together, and as Bridey leaned against Canola

97

she felt her mood lighten and her anger go as quickly as it had appeared.

"Can we help?" she asked politely, but Tahan waved her away and continued to clear leaves and inks and scraps of parchment from the table. He went over to a small fire that glowed in the corner and came back carrying a large steaming pot, and the girls realised how hungry they were; Bridey had had nothing since breakfast, and Canola had eaten little but dry bread in five days. Their mouths watered and they eagerly accepted the bowls of stew. Tahan watched them eat, studying their faces. He began to speak.

"Yes, Fionnuala was right – it is a striking likeness. One as dark as the night, the other fair as the sun. She must have brought you together for some reason." The girls looked up, their mouths full, but the old man continued, his voice thoughtful. "The trees are almost bare now, and the wind has a rattling sound. The hives are asleep too . . . what can she want, so late in the year?"

Bridey swallowed.

"Who, Master? Mother Abbess?" But Tahan chuckled and shook his head.

"No, no, not Fionnuala! Goodness, no . . ."

"Then who?" The back of Bridey's neck was prickling, and she could feel Canola bolt upright beside her. Bridey felt the crown where it lay, deep in the pocket of her cloak.

Tahan hummed for a moment and tapped lightly on his drum. Ignoring Bridey's question, he rose and consulted a smudged chart that hung on the dusty wall, and the girls watched his bent finger as it travelled lightly across the lines and diagrams. "Three days!" he declared, turning to them. "If I'm not mistaken, we have three days left before the year is out. Now, where is the moon?" and he stared blankly about as if expecting to find it in the little room.

Once again Canola felt laughter rising, and she bit hard upon the cloth of her sleeve. This time she felt Bridey rocking silently against her, and she dared not look. Apparently unaware, Tahan once again stuck his head out of the window.

Bridey breathed deeply and composed herself.

"He knows about B-Brigit, doesn't he?" she whispered urgently.

"I don't know," muttered Canola, "it's hard to . . ." and she subsided helplessly.

Tahan turned from the window and said, "You have a journey to make. I heard it in the last leaves. Brigit has been angered by kings and warriors, by foolish men and their foolish boasting; now she has unsheathed her own sword. But I wonder why she should have chosen you and the young poet to do her bidding?" He shrugged and stared at the sky.

Bridey put a hand in her pocket and felt the cold smoothness of Brigit's crown. She wished she had never seen it. It did not belong to her. Suddenly she knew what to do. On the eve of Samain, when the Tuatha dé Danaan walked once more from their long barrows, she must find the Goddess Brigit and restore to her the golden crown of power.

Tahan said, "You've wasted enough time already. Blood is being spilled while you delay. Soon there will be no stopping it. Myself, I want to get some sleep tonight. Now, tell me, what are your questions? I am too old for most things, but I still have my uses. Go on, ask! What do you need to know?"

Canola stared, her mouth open foolishly.

"Go on," she nudged Bridey.

"I . . . er . . ."

Tahan's hand rapped on his drum. Suddenly he looked tired and impatient, no longer a benevolent old man.

"We need to know about the Tomb of Reeds," Bridey said. "Do you know what it is? And where? Perhaps you have a map?"

Immediately Tahan turned away to bend down and scrabble about among the bundles of parchment under his bed. They could hear him muttering in annoyance. "A map, is it? Just like that! A map, please, Tahan, if you'd be so kind . . ." and he straightened up slowly. "So you want to look for the barrows of the Tuatha? You want to search among the dead? Well, be careful – they're no more reliable than the living. Here . . ." and he thrust a dirty rag towards Bridey. She just had time to grasp the piece of dirty deerskin, before she and Canola were unceremoniously bundled out of the door.

". . . and go to sleep!" were his last words, and they blinked at each other in surprise. The light went out and they were left in darkness. The moon was hidden behind a bank of cloud and they could not even make out each other's faces in the gloom.

"What shall we do?" hissed Canola.

"We . . ."

Bridey yawned and realised how sleepy she was. She supposed she should go home, taking Canola, but it was too dark, and she was too tired.

"Come on," she whispered, and felt for Canola's hand.

As the moon slid from behind the clouds they could just make out Ceibhfhionn where she stood, tethered to a log. They stumbled towards her and together they managed to pull off the saddle. Taking a blanket from the saddlebag, they wrapped themselves up in it and settled down together among the leaves. Bridey looked up once more at the moon and the waving treetops, and then her eyes became too heavy. Moving closer to Canola she quickly fell asleep.

They awoke at dawn to find Tahan was gone, but next to Ceibhfhionn stood a black pony which Bridey recognised as one of the convent horses. The old druid must have fetched him before daybreak. The pony was saddled and equipped for a journey, with food and blankets, and he snorted eagerly as Bridey stroked his neck. Both girls looked round the empty glade. The path that led from the settlement seemed to beckon them.

"Are we supposed to go alone?" asked Canola.

"There's no one else," said Bridey.

Ceibhfhionn lifted her head and whinnied as Canola hoisted on the saddle and tightened the girth. The horse's keenness infected the girls. What lay before them was unknown and dangerous. They wanted to stay, but itched to be gone.

Before she climbed into the saddle, Bridey dug in her pocket and found the map that Tahan had given her the night before. She spread it out on the black pony's rump and she and Canola peered at it hopefully. At first it was nothing but a confusing network, then slowly shapes emerged. They saw the land open up – the wide sea, the ragged coastline, bleak plains and rugged highlands.

They mounted the restless ponies and prepared to set off east. As they trotted away from the glade Canola gave a hollow laugh. It was the same as when she had left Corkaguiney: it felt like there was a slender line between adventure and sheer folly. She tried to summon a fragment of verse, some doggerel to lighten their mood, but nothing came to her and she kept silent.

"I'm scared, Bridey . . ." she admitted finally. "I don't want to go."

They looked back. Behind them lay the peaceful settlement, the convent, the farmland – not wholly safe, but safer than what lay ahead. Bridey, feeling the golden crown digging into her hip, reached over and clasped her hand.

"We'll be back," she assured Canola. "My mother will miss me. And I never said goodbye to Eadha."

Canola had nothing to say. Resolutely she set her face forward and kicked Ceibhfhionn into a trot, following Bridey's black pony. Together, frightened and filled with uncertainty, the girls rode deeper into the woods.

11. eastwards

I am the giant who wields a sharp sword ...

The day was dull and windy, with bare branches swaying bleakly overhead; even the birds seemed affected, rarely calling through the damp woods. But nothing managed to dull Bridey's growing sense of excitement. She had never been beyond the boundaries of the settlement before. The woodlands about the convent clearing were familiar and safe, but these were new woods, overgrown and dark. They smelled different, sounded different – they were dangerous and unexplored. It was like taking the coracle over the lake and steering too near the current. The black pony was lively, and the sheer act of riding through the woods elated her and her misgivings disappeared.

Canola caught Bridey's mood. The more buoyant of the two, she soon settled back to enjoy herself, laughing and talking and keeping up a stream of jokes and observations. Bridey listened fitfully, her thoughts drifting. She half mistrusted her happiness, forcing herself to keep an eye out for anything unusual or threatening, but they did not see a soul or pass a dwelling all morning. Hour after hour they rode through forest where nothing changed but the trees. The oaks thinned out and were replaced by beech, then for ten miles on either side were groves of ancient yews, growing so densely that the air was still and thick, and the girls spoke in whispers. By noon they had left the forest and only a few stunted rowans grew in clumps among heather and naked rock.

They had travelled fast, trotting for long stretches where the road was good, resting the ponies when it became uneven and strewn with rocks. It was hard to know how many miles they had covered, for at times the road twisted and turned and they lost all sense of direction. When the sun finally broke through the thick cloud, Bridey reckoned it must be midday.

"Ouch! I suppose you're used to this," she said, rubbing her bottom and wriggling in the saddle. "I'm stiff all over, and hungry, too."

"I think we could risk a short break," said Canola, laughing at Bridey's contortions. She swung down and tied Ceibhfhionn to a bush. Bridey slithered down awkwardly, her legs jelly.

They found newly baked bread, dried fish and a jar of honey in Bridey's saddlebag, and it seemed like a feast as they munched the bread and drank water from the wineskins, feeling surprisingly light-hearted. It was peaceful, sitting in the feeble sunshine, but they were nearing the border country and could not forget the danger. They finished eating and consulted the map.

The road led east across a wide plain. Far away, among the eastern marshes, lay the Tomb of Reeds, their mysterious destination, drawn on the map with double spirals of thick black ink. To the north were the mountains, a smudge of blue on the horizon; to the south lay peat-bogs and more marshes.

They decided to keep to the road for a few more miles, surely no enemy soldiers could have come this far west. If it got more dangerous later on they would take the smaller road further south. Neither relished taking the ponies into the treacherous bogs; they could see them, miles away, brilliant green – beautiful from a distance, but in reality brackish and swarming with midges.

Canola wrinkled her nose and looked about thoughtfully.

"It's hard," she said.

"What is?"

"It's hard to believe in the war, it's so quiet here. Why should anyone want to spoil this quietness? I suppose it *is* real?"

"Remember the battlefield," said Bridey, untying the black pony, ". . . and poor Cormac."

She climbed into the saddle. This pony may not be the tall

steed of a war-lord, but he was a sight better than Cron. All gloomy thoughts disappeared as she nudged him forward and cantered away, fixing her concentration on the road that wound ahead through the heather.

Towards evening both girls were tired, nodding sleepily in the saddle but determined not to rest until the light had gone. Behind them the sun sank slowly in the sky, staining the clouds a lurid crimson. The land all about was blackened and scorched, though whether from war or from summer fires they could not tell. The gnarled bushes rattled in the wind and Bridey and Canola wrapped themselves snugly in their cloaks. Both thought of food and a warm bed.

Canola had been entertaining Bridey all day with snatches of songs and elaborate reminiscences. She had no scruple about bending the truth and Bridey often exclaimed in disbelief at some new piece of exaggeration. Canola told of her journey from Corkaguiney, her voice flat and monotonous as she described the forest and farmlands, but rising high and dramatic when she spoke of wolves heard in the night and wild boars glimpsed rooting in the earth only yards from where she slept.

"What did you do?"

"Oh, I climbed a tree and waited a while, then sang a song until the old boar went to sleep. Then I climbed down again and tied a piece of pink ribbon round his tusk, to remind him of me when he woke . . ."

"You liar!"

"Not at all," insisted Canola, annoyed that Bridey could see no difference between fact and rhetoric.

But Bridey was beginning to see that much of Canola's talk was simply a pleasant noise that filled the silence. It did not hide her nervousness and often Bridey wished she would be quiet. By the evening she had begun to counter Canola's chatter calmly, and they were able to continue in companionable silence. Bridey no longer felt so dull and stolid beside Canola's wit and airiness. Away from the settlement she was more confident and self-contained.

Canola was aware of her nervousness, so she shrouded herself with puns and satire, hating the sound of her own voice jabbering on like a magpie, but she was unable to stop the endless cleverness. In Corkaguiney she was encouraged to be loquacious. Wit and satire, the crueller the better, were the tools of a poet's trade, and the young apprentices were being groomed for when they would take their places at court, and perhaps even sit at the table of the King. Canola had never questioned the value of it before, but now, beside Bridey, she saw her own brilliance as nothing more than froth – as vapid as the bubbles on beer. Why couldn't she be more like Bridey, whose words were sensible and solid?

As evening drew in, all that could be heard was the clop of the horses' feet and the call of a late bird. The sun finally sank below the horizon as they passed through a place of such desolation that they drew together and cast furtive looks left and right.

It was a deserted settlement: broken walls, heaped ash where the huts had stood, blackened fences . . . and in the centre, the tall charred roof beams of the church where the people had gathered to celebrate their festivals. There was nothing else left. If there had been a massacre there was no sign of it – no rotting bodies, no blood . . . nothing . . . only the sad ghosts of the people which slid into shadows as the girls rode by. High overhead flew the barnacle geese, moving steadily south to spend the winter feeding in the marshlands. Flock after flock passed over, the sound of their wings like the beat of a drum.

Bridey looked back at the burnt-out houses. She saw the timbers of the church – stark black lines against the sky – and she was frightened, not merely of unseen enemies, but of whatever it was in men that made them indulge in such wastefulness. What courage had it taken to destroy an undefended collection of farms?

Canola trembled. Fear was like a giant crouching in the darkness behind her, a malevolent giant with an ugly club and hands that loved squeezing the breath from his victims. She was shaking. What had led her to believe that she would be spared? How arrogant! What made her different from these people whose existence had been so casually snuffed out?

A screech from behind caused them both to cry out. They spun round to see what had made such a terrible sound.

"Aiee-hah-haha!"

It was no animal that confronted them, but a woman. She was naked, save for a torn and dirty cloak, and her feet were bruised and bare. Her hair hung lank and colourless; bloody patches showed where it had been wrenched out in clumps.

"Aah-ha! ha! ha! . . ." she howled. Bridey and Canola looked at each other in horror, then back at the women. Instinctively Bridey waited, expecting Canola to make the first move, but Canola was paralysed. She would rather see a hundred dead bodies than this one ravaged, living person. She backed Ceibhfhionn away, shrinking from any contact, terrified in case the woman touched her.

So it was Bridey who dismounted and approached the woman, holding out her hand.

"Here . . . come here," she called softly. "It's all right. Don't be scared."

The woman bared her teeth and bent to pick up a stone.

"Get away from me," she snarled, and rushed at Bridey. She looked savage, but at the last moment she darted away again, too afraid to throw the stone, and collapsed on the ground. "No, don't," she pleaded. "Go away, soldier."

"I'm not a soldier," said Bridey. "Look . . ." and again she held out her hands, "we're girls." But the woman backed away, snuffling and mumbling nonsensically.

"They split the milk, all the milk, all over the ground . . . never mind, we'll clear it up, lovey, but don't let them see you . . . Oh, all the poor chickens, all my chicks . . ."

Bridey looked at Canola, but the poet looked away and shrugged.

"Who did this?" Bridey asked. "Who burnt the huts? Where are the people? Why have you stayed?"

The woman gave another hoarse sobbing laugh.

"Have you lost your wits, girl? Don't tell me you haven't seen them. They're crawling over the land like rats. They're every-where, killing us all. Why have you been spared, if my girls were not?" Suddenly she did not look mad at all, only beaten. "You must be Tarans, to have been left alone. I don't care any longer . . . you have taken all I ever had."

"So it was the Tarans who . . ."

"Pah!" The woman spat on the ground and Bridey stared at the spittle in fascination. "The men of Tara? Yes, it was them who burnt us out. But before that it was Breagh's brave warriors who stole our food, and our boys, our men . . ." She fell to her knees and beat the ground weakly with her fists. "The foolish men! Why did they go? The cowards . . . They left so happily! Went to bereave Taran women, I suppose. Yes, *they* must be made to grieve too." She gave a vicious laugh. "Are Taran women being left alone, with their harvest stolen and their houses burnt? I hope so."

There was a horrible silence. Crows hopped among the ashes.

"Come with us," Bridey beckoned. "We'll take you to where it's safe. Are you hungry? We can help you."

"Nowhere's safe, fool," hissed the woman, "and I can't leave. My girls will be coming back. They went to the church to hide," and she pointed a grimy finger at the charred ruin behind her. "They'll be back in a while, I must wait for them." Turning, she walked off, her bare feet careless of the spiked burnt earth.

Canola coughed.

"We'll leave some food for her, Bridey."

Bridey looked up blankly.

"She could be my mother," she said.

Canola said nothing, but dismounted and began to take some bread from the saddlebag. She carried it over to where a well stood in the middle of the ruined huts. Here a few tufts of grass remained, the only sign of life. She brushed clear a piece of the flagstone and put down the bread. She was desperate to be gone, but she forced herself to make slow measured movements. Behind her the woman called, "Run away if you know what's good for you. The raven will be back for her pickings," and Canola remembered the riddle on the beech block: 'The Raven croaks and death is all about . . .'

They left her crouched near the gutted church. She called after them jeeringly, and her voice joined with the cawing of the crows.

The sun was gone but some light still remained, and wanting to be far away from this place before dark, they urged their ponies forward into the gloom, making their way along a ridge of high ground that ran across the plain. Stunted trees grew on the slopes, and streams ran south through rocky gullies to join the watery marshland. Foxes barked and the girls shivered. At last, when the ponies were no longer sure of their footing, they stopped in the shadow of a high cliff where they tethered the ponies and made a fire. There was no shortage of wood, rotten branches lay scattered at the base of the cliff, and handfuls of dry moss could be pulled from the stone for kindling.

"Do you think we should?" asked Bridey. "It might not be safe. Someone might see."

They stopped and listened, but after a minute, when all they heard was the stream that ran below the cliff, they built the fire high. They could not bear to be without its comfort that night.

As Bridey rummaged in her saddlebag for their provisions, she found something which made her exclaim with delight. At the bottom of the bag, wrapped in a piece of rough sacking, were ten fat white candles, the kind the Abbess used to light her sanctuary. She felt Fionnuala's sturdy presence and remembered the yellow light falling on the old tapestries. She brought out the candles and paused to consider: should she light one or two? Then she laughed. What was the use of saving? They had two days, no more, and she wanted to perform a piece of humble magic. Taking a burning twig from the fire, she lit all ten candles and planted them in a wide circle in the ground.

"Oh, that's good," said Canola when she came back with an armful of wood and saw the circle of light enclosing their fire.

"There's nothing like a circle for keeping out the wolves. If we're going to meet the Tuatha we must make sure we're not eaten first."

They ate bread and honey and apples that were wrinkled but still sweet, and talked in low voices. When they had finished Canola got up and fetched her harp from the saddlebag.

"We may as well have a little music."

As they sat and warmed themselves by the fire, Canola softly sang airs and lullabies, her fingers wandering over the strings. When she sang of Tir inna mBan, the Land of Women, Bridey recognised the words and joined in, hesitant at first, but gaining confidence as Canola nodded encouragement.

> *Tir inna mBan, the distant isle,*
> *Where sea-horses glisten with dragonstones,*
> *Fair course on which the white waves surge,*
> *Four pedestals upholding.*
>
> *There, there is neither 'mine' nor 'thine',*
> *White are the teeth there, dark the brow;*
> *Purple the surface of every plain,*
> *A marvel of beauty the blackbird's egg ...*

Their singing gave them back the strength they had lost during the day, the courage that had been sapped by the sight of the burned settlement and its only survivor. When Canola finally laid down the harp and curled up beside Bridey, both girls had lulled themselves into peacefulness. As the fire died to glowing embers, they quickly fell asleep, lit by candles.

12. the anchorite

I am the salmon in a dark pool . . .

The next morning as the sky lightened, Bridey was making her way along the banks of the stream in the shadow of the overhanging cliff. She had left Canola cooking the fish they had caught and now she was following the stream to see where it led. Was it a tributary of the river that lay across their path? If so, to follow it would be a shortcut of ten miles or more, and certainly safer than going by road, though there was still no sign of life in the bleak landscape. Only a few ducks rose clattering from the water when they heard her footsteps.

The stream was widening; surely around the next bend she would see the broad sweep of the river. If the current was not too fast it should be possible to cross it with the ponies. She went on, keeping to the rocks. Her dreams had been full of soldiers and wild-eyed kings riding over the bodies of her family. First Sorcha, then her mother had been among the dead, staring up at her with cold, unseeing eyes. She had woken with a shout and she and Canola had huddled together to wait for the dawn, too scared to sleep. As she moved through the mist, her body ached and her eyelids drooped. Beneath her breath she hummed a fragment of last night's song over and over, the same six notes, mechanical and soothing . . .

Seeing the stream veer to the left, she clambered up the slope and looked around. There was the river, wide and grey, with white mist curling over its surface. Without waiting she turned and ran back the way she had come.

"The river's just round the corner," she said, arriving back to the smell of cooked fish and the sight of Canola's anxious face.

"It's much quicker, look . . . " and she ran her finger over the lines on the creased and grubby map.

"We'll be better away from the road," agreed Canola, spearing a fish with her knife.

They ate quickly. A sense of urgency hung over them, making the food stick in their throats. Destroying all evidence of the fire, they set off over the tangled headland, leading the ponies through the brambles and creepers that festooned the stunted trees. It was hard going, and they were exhausted by the time they had broken through and saw the river gleaming below them.

"I hope it's easier from here on," gasped Canola, ripping a bramble from around her waist and soothing Ceibhfhionn who was dancing backwards in protest.

"It should be, there's a path down there," Bridey pointed.

"But there are no farms near here," said Canola. "Who could have made it? Sheep, perhaps?"

Bridey was hot and worried. Canola, for all her verbal ingenuity, seemed to be leaving most of the decisions to her, and Bridey hated making decisions; they gave her a feeling of panic.

Canola was tired and angry, and thought that Bridey was being unreasonable. Every time she made a suggestion, Bridey rejected it and made her feel a fool. They were both frightened and irritable. The map was almost impossible to follow, and once again the sun was hidden in thick cloud, so they could not easily tell in which direction they were travelling.

"I suppose it's safe."

"We don't have much of a choice."

Bridey started down the slope, pulling the unwilling black pony, and Canola trailed after her, singing a song to try to raise their spirits. Half-way down Bridey turned and crossly told her to be quiet. Canola flushed and fell silent.

They crashed noisily to the bottom and eventually reached the path a few yards from where the river flowed. Bridey got out the map and pored over it, while Canola stood nearby, whistling softly and looking at the sky. There was an unfrien-

dly silence, then Bridey said, "I think there are shallows
further down, we should cross there." She looked up. "What
do you think?"

"Who, me?" asked Canola with a tight smile. "Oh, indeed,
cross further down. We don't want to get swept away, do we?"

Bridey shrugged.

"We've got to be careful, and we've got so little time." Their
task loomed before them and she wanted to say, "What will we
do? It's impossible. I don't understand," but she could not,
and instead said clumsily, "Please, w-we must hurry," and her
words sounded curt and unnecessary. "C-come on."

Canola smiled fixedly.

"Very well," she said. "After you, willow-woman, I'm sure
you swim as beautifully as you sing." Spitefully she began to
murmur to herself in the old language of the bards, knowing
Bridey could not understand. She hated herself for the way she
was being, but she hated Bridey too.

Bridey flushed and swore beneath her breath. Her eyes were
hot and sore and she could hear Canola whispering the
unknown words, as sharp as a knife. Suddenly they were
enemies. Saying nothing she began to march up the path with
the black pony trotting behind her, grateful to be out of the
brambles.

Canola followed, her chest tight and constricted. She wanted
to push Bridey into the river, to slap her, insult her and make
her sorry, but she also wanted to run and catch her arm, make
up, be friends again. How strange, she thought: to like and
hate at the same time.

They marched for a mile beside the river, the distance
between them growing. Bridey walked with her eyes fixed on
the ground, careless of danger now. Her mind was a fog of
ill-feeling and her thoughts were as bleak as the landscape.
Suddenly her way was barred by a tall pillar of stone. It was
covered with ivy and decorated with spirals and at the top was
a crude cross. It looked hundreds of years old, worn and
weatherbeaten. Bridey glanced back and saw Canola waiting,
one eyebrow raised. Canola's face was like a mirror held up to

mock her, and she hated the white hair and the disdainful mouth. Pulling at the bridle, Bridey began to edge round the lump of stone.

The black pony objected. Maybe he did not like squeezing so close to the cliff, or perhaps the pillar seemed sinister to him. Either way he reared up and plunged backwards, tugging the reins from Bridey's hand. She shouted in alarm and waved her arms, frightening him further. Canola saw the pony wheel and canter away, leaving Bridey in the shadow of the standing stone. She wanted to help, but hurt pride held her back. As Bridey began to trudge after the pony, Canola saw a tall figure step out from behind the stone.

"Bridey, look out!"

Bridey turned and Canola ran forward. Bridey had her willow-cutting knife in her hand.

The man was tall and very thin. He wore a simple robe of coarse cloth that fell from his bony shoulders to the ground. In one hand he carried a fishing line, in the other a tattered book, and his eyes glittered in his gaunt face as he stared at the two young people who were trespassing on his riverbank.

"Why are you here? Do you come in peace," he looked at Bridey's knife, "or with a sword?" His accent was strange, his voice high and urgent, and Bridey and Canola moved together, their bad temper forgotten. When they did not reply, the man passed a hand across his eyes and repeated the question.

"Why are you here? Are you real, or mere shadows?" He turned his face and looked at the sky. "Oh, demon or temptress, whichever you are : here are surely two in one . . . light and shade . . . two sides of a coin, both uppermost," and his eyes travelled from Bridey to Canola and back again.

Canola cleared her throat and motioned to Bridey to put away her knife.

"Are you guardian of the stone, Master?" she said formally. "If so, give us leave to pass unhindered, for we bear no arms, nor malice, neither." This was the way to address him, she supposed, for he must be a holy man, and this was how Liadan spoke to the wandering monks who sometimes passed through

Corkaguiney asking for food and shelter. Connacht was full of them. They walked northwards, sometimes in pairs but often alone, carrying the new faiths to scattered farmsteads. They were messengers from overseas, passionate converts whom many dismissed as obscure cultists, but others revered as sages. Often they would build a little hut of stone in some wild and dangerous spot, and spend their time in fasting and meditation and mysterious alchemical research.

Bridey spoke.

"We are t-travellers whose mission is perilous. Show us where to ford the river in safety and we will g-go." Copying Canola she raised her hand to make, on her palm, the sign of the fish – the sign of safe passage.

"Pass, by all means," said the man, scratching his thin bearded cheek, "but there is no safety on the other side. The land is all about ravaged by war, and angels weep in pity at the slaughter."

"Are the armies nearby?" asked Bridey. "And King Breagh? Have you news of the King?"

The man stared at them wildly.

"My King is not upon this earth," he replied. "He reigns on high. He is the Magician, the Alpha and the Omega. He will come with the clouds, in his right hand seven stars, in his mouth a sharp sword. He is my bread and my light . . . " and he brandished his tattered book and lapsed into a lilting language.

"Goodness," said Canola, "Greek!" and she cocked her head to listen. She knew too little and could catch only the odd syllable.

"But King Breagh," pursued Bridey, "what about him?"

"Breagh serves the Beast," the man declared in a contemptuous voice. "He gathers his men, promising them the flesh of mighty men and captains. But he is a fool. The Tarans are coming sevenfold, and the Queen of Heaven will split the world asunder. Tomorrow is the day the graves will yawn and the dead will walk abroad. We must do their will . . . or else all Erin will be drowned beneath a tide of blood."

"Do you understand any of this?" whispered Bridey.

"No, I wish he'd be more specific," and Canola drew a deep breath. "Master, have you seen soldiers hereabouts? Men on horses?"

"I see a pale horse and his name is Death."

The man waved his battered book at them and a few crumpled pages fell to the ground and blew across the shingle. Bridey and Canola ran to pick them up, and Canola sighed as she plucked a sheet of paper from a bramble.

"These mystics," she muttered, "there's no sense in them at all." She handed back the missing page, then said loudly, "Well, well, we shall just have to chance our luck on the highway."

"No, no, you cannot use the road. It's swarming with mercenaries. I don't know which side they belong to, but it makes no difference – they're holding the land to ransom and the people are fleeing." His hands twitched and his brow puckered with irritation. "Come with me," he said. "I'll show you the way, but heaven knows why you want to go east, straight towards the soldiers."

"But where exactly *are* they?" asked Bridey again. "Could you show us – we have a map," and she fumbled in her pocket. But the man was striding away and they had to run back to fetch the ponies. They hurried after him along the narrow path, and this time both ponies passed the standing stone without protest.

A quarter of a mile along the river stood the hermit's dwelling. It was a tall curved structure, like the beehive cells in Fionnuala's convent, but built entirely of slate and rocks, without even a window or a chimney. Here the river was deep and dangerous, and the cliffs towered on either side. A hundred yards further on it widened and became shallow and quiet.

"There is the place," cried the man, and walking into the river until it was up to his knees, he began crying in a loud voice. "And the music of harps, and of flutes, and of trumpets shall be silenced. And so it shall be until Hades surrenders the dead. Then Death itself shall be cast into a lake of fire ... ." The skirts of his robe floated about his knees, and he lowered his voice

and asked, "But why all this urgency? What could be so important that you must ride into a hostile land? Poetry and laughter
are dying every day while Brigit rages and the King roars."

Canola shivered.

"We must leave," she said, nudging Bridey, and quickly they
mounted the ponies and began to pick their way along the river
bank towards the place where they could cross. Behind them
the man in the river was calling out, splashing his head and
beating the water with his fists.

"Remember this . . . remember my words: the world is one
soul, with no division. Take white garments to hide yourselves
. . . white robes dipped in blood . . . " His voice faded as they
rode away and was soon lost in the sound of the river.

Bridey laughed nervously.

"Do you think he's mad?"

"Moonstruck," replied Canola decisively. "They're all the
same, these zealots – mad as March hares and twice as touchy."

Bridey chuckled. She looked at the river dubiously.

"Time to get our feet wet."

"You first, then."

The ponies, who had been drinking deeply, lifted their heads
and looked over the river. The far banks were thick with gorse
and bracken, unwelcoming, but with a narrow overgrown path
winding up the slope.

"That's the way." Canola nudged Ceibhfhionn into the river.

The water was viciously cold. The ponies snorted and
floundered and threatened to throw them off. The current
tugged at the girl's legs, but they clung on, lying along the
ponies' necks, and soon they were in the shallows on the other
side. They splashed forward, patting the ponies. Every trace of
bad feeling had gone. They were frozen, but reunited.

Clattering over the shingle, they were just about to start
along the rough track through the bracken when a movement
glimpsed out of the corner of her eye caused Bridey to turn her
head. For a moment she could not speak, and when she did her
voice was full of anger and astonishment.

"Eadha! What are you doing here?"

13. eaoha

I am the shield for every heart ...

"Come on, speak up! How did you get here?" Bridey was furious and frightened. She did not even get off her pony, but stayed looming over her terrified brother, her face red with anger. Eadha cowered back under a bush, wincing at every word, and it was Canola who dismounted and went over to him, speaking gently.

"Well, Eadha," she said, "what a surprise. Have you followed us all the way from home? It's a long way." She spoke cheerfully and gave him a smile, but his eyes were wide and staring. He was drenched and shivering and his black hair was smeared across his face. "Did you cross the river, then? Did you swim?"

Eadha's face crumpled and he burst into tears. The sight of his sister's face, so stern and appalling, was too much for him. Now this strange poet, with a face so like Bridey's, was reaching out to him and gently pulling him from his hiding place. He kicked feebly with his legs and sobbed, woeful and embarrassed. He had pictured himself riding up bravely in the nick of time and rescuing his sister from some danger or other; he had sustained himself with thoughts of her gratitude, of how happy she would be to see him. Now it had all gone wrong. He was speechless with fear. Bridey was angry and hateful; Cron was gone ... At the thought of the old brown pony, Eadha choked with misery. His shoulders heaved and his nose began to run.

Bridey watched as he kicked weakly at Canola, resisting her attempts to comfort him. She clambered down, and going slowly to where he sat, leaned in front of Canola and took him in her arms, rocking him back and forth, holding him close as she had always done if he fell and grazed his knee or ran to her after a fight with his friends.

"Shh, shh . . . it's all right now. Stop crying and tell me what happened. Don't worry," she added untruthfully, "I'm not cross."

Canola stood back and watched as Bridey calmly stopped Eadha's tears. She had no little brother herself, but had often longed for one. She could barely remember her older brothers – boys with half-forgotten faces, who excluded her from their games, and who had been sent away, like herself, in the early morning. At Corkaguiney there had been the other poets, but none of them were close to her. Then, for a while, there had been Bridey . . . but now, with Eadha here, that would change. She felt hollow inside.

Bridey wiped Eadha's face with her cuff, and made him blow his nose. Soon the boy was able to speak, though from time to time his eyes filled with tears. He felt stronger with Bridey's arms around him.

"I knew you'd gone," he said. "I went and looked in your bed, and you hadn't been back. I thought you were captured or eaten by a wolf, but then I heard Mother talking to the Abbess, so I knew you'd run off . . . and it's not fair. It's my crown too!"

He had been hanging out of the little window in the loft, where he slept with the onions, listening to his mother and Fionnuala talking down below. It was easy to hear them for their voices had been loud and disagreeable.

"But she *had* to go, don't you understand? It was foretold in the sticks. She had something important to do, and we could not keep her from it." This was the Abbess, her voice insistent. "You know what she's been like recently. We couldn't help."

"Why? What could be so important that it needs a child? She's just a child! What can she do? It's ridiculous. It's to do with that ash-headed poet, isn't it? I knew I should have kept them apart."

"It's out of our hands, my child," the Abbess said. "You must give her your blessing."

"No! I don't understand what's wrong with the world. I've no young man to lose, so they take my daughter."

"Yes, thankfully Eadha's too young," murmured the Abbess. "Remember, Bridey has not gone to take lives, my child. She is trying to stop the fighting – so the sons can come home."

They moved away and Eadha heard no more. He knew only that his sister had gone, taking the road east with the young poet, and travelling towards danger. He knew how unhappy she had been ever since Midsummer ... ever since he had shown her the crown, his crown. It must be something to do with that. If so, then it was his journey too. He would not be left at home like a baby.

What had his mother thought when she called him to breakfast and he was nowhere to be found? He was eight years old, and only thought of himself and how he was going to help his sister. He did not think of his mother's desperation when she realised that another of her children had ridden off towards war.

He trotted through the woods on Cron's broad back, his head full of stories of great danger and feats of outstanding courage. He would rescue King Breagh from a Taran ambush, he would capture enemy soldiers and meet princes and slay dragons. He had missed the return of Gegra and the other men because his mother had kept him indoors churning butter, so war for Eadha was still a game, a celebration, a colourful adventure – not a bleak reality.

By nightfall, when he had still not caught up with Bridey and Canola, Eadha found himself full of fear and empty-bellied, without even a crust of bread for comfort. He had finished his provisions before even leaving the forest. He kept following the road and by the time he passed through the burnt-out settlement he was terrified and miserable. Hearing faint cries and screams coming from the ruined church, he had bolted, kicking Cron into a jolting canter. He was unable to find his sister and her friend and had not the slightest idea of where to look for them. He had thought he could track them, but one bruised blade of grass was much like another and the road was pitted with old hoof-prints.

Then it was dark.

He and Cron had spent the night in a dense thicket, and were woken the next morning by harsh shouts and a loud crashing nearby. Cowering beside the fat pony, Eadha watched as twenty armed men slashed their way through the undergrowth only yards from where he stood. Who were they? He assumed they were Tarans, the bloody enemy, who had teeth like wolves and eyes that shone in the dark; who ate human flesh and whose shields bore the sign of the crow. As he clung to Cron's saddle, the boy managed to open his eyes wide enough to catch a glimpse of the men who blundered past.

They were ugly and brutal, with faces full of anger and impatience as they fought through the bushes, swearing and pulling their horses behind them, snagging their fur-lined cloaks on the thorns. Cron had lifted his nose to greet the war-horses and Eadha clutched at the brown muzzle. "No . . . no," he whispered, and Cron stayed quiet, only pricking his ears in curiosity at the noisy progress of the soldiers.

They passed by without seeing the boy and the brown pony, and it was not until the last soldier kicked his way through and disappeared over the brow of the hill that Eadha noticed, slung across the man's shoulder, a round shield. He gasped. This was not the shield of a Taran: instead of a crow, it bore the emblem of a prancing horse.

These were men of Connacht.

How angry and malevolent they looked; he could not imagine them sending him a friendly greeting, or reaching down to pull him into the saddle. He was amazed and confounded: they were as frightening as the Tarans. What was the difference?

An hour passed before he dared venture from his hiding place, then he scrambled onto Cron and kicked the pony into a shambling trot. Another hour and he came to the banks of a fast flowing river.

Eadha's hectic narrative came to an end and he stared at Bridey and Canola with round eyes. The first part of his story had been bearable, the second was not.

"What happened then?" Bridey demanded.

"We tried to cross," he said in a small voice, "but it was too deep."

He remembered the pull of the current and the numbing cold, and his fear as the water closed over his head and his fingers were torn from Cron's mane. The pony had kicked and struggled, trying to make headway in the freezing current, but helplessly, and with increasing weakness. They were swept along for several miles, until Eadha was at last washed up on the shingle of the shallows. But Cron was carried on.

Bridey struggled with tears. She had abused the old pony so many times, cursing his fatness and lack of speed, wishing he was a proper horse – but she had loved him too.

"Poor old pony," said Canola, who had come to listen. "Never mind, Eadha, he'll go straight to the Isles of the Blessed. He died in a good brave cause." She tilted her head and recited a poem about the paradise of Tir Nan Og, the land beyond the sunset where heroes and horses go after their death; where harps play themselves and flowers bloom all the year round. All the time she spoke, Canola remembered the bloated bodies of the battlefields, and wondered why she was lying to the child: a dead horse was no more than a piece of rotting flesh, a dead man the same.

> "... *and noble horses end their weary days*
> *In pastures green, beneath St. Brigit's gaze.*

For no one dies, you know," she added self-consciously. "Not really. Not even fat ponies."

Eadha cheered up. He looked at Bridey and Canola and began to ask a stream of questions.

"Where are you going? What are you going to do? What have you done with the crown? You should have asked me to come . . ." His voice sank reproachfully.

"It's too dangerous," said Bridey, "but now you're here I

suppose you'll have to stay." Then she blurted, "Why do you always have to interfere? I thought for once I'd actually got away from you." She could not help it, her family intruded even here, in the middle of nowhere. "Promise not to get in the way." Seeing Eadha's face, she immediately felt guilty.

He was scowling and tearful. "It's not fair, I'm old enough. I won't do anything stupid."

The girls looked at each other and sighed, but Eadha had not finished.

"What are you going to do? Why don't you tell me?" He prodded Bridey's arm, "Are you taking the crown to the King, to help him win the war?"

Canola snorted.

"Breagh has no need of Brigit's crown! He needs new wits, perhaps! Taking on the Tarans, indeed, and ruining the harvest. There's one way to lose your friends . . ." She carried on muttering to herself, suddenly full of resentment. Who was this new King to expect everyone to drop what they were doing and rush to do his bidding?

"Is it Brigit's crown, then?" asked the boy.

"As far as we know," nodded Bridey. "Canola's got a riddle that tells us what to do."

"When Aspen, born of Willow, wets his feet . . ." Canola recited the riddle while Eadha listened, putting his head on one side and furrowing his brow. When the poem was over and Canola was murmuring to herself the few words she could not understand, he looked from one to the other and said in a solemn voice, "So, we have to find Brigit and give it back to her."

The girls threw back their heads and laughed.

"Just like that!"

Bridey got up and walked away. Her shoes squelched. "I hope the sun comes out, or we'll catch our death. Come on, we must go. Eadha, you ride with me." She hoisted the boy onto the black pony and climbed up after him. Within a few minutes they were making their way up the narrow path that led through the trees.

Eight hours later they had followed the path as far as it went. It had led them through scrubland and over rough pasture where a few wild sheep scattered at their approach. Now it petered out near the ruins of an ancient sheep-cote on exposed hillside, and from where they stood they could see the road winding east across the plain to Tara. They consulted the map and saw that their way led across the moor. At some point they must cross the road, but not before dark. Bridey had the keenest eyes of the three and she could see horsemen moving like flies along the line of the road, some going east, some west. Who were they? From such a distance it was impossible to tell.

The sun came out as the ponies plodded steadily over the rough turf, following a line of low trees that shielded them from the road. At the bottom of the hill was a farmstead, and as they passed by, watching carefully for any movement, they saw that it had been deserted. Only a half-starved dog scratched about in the dust.

"Are there ghosts here?" hissed Eadha, peering back over his shoulder, but both girls shrugged and neither spoke. Who could say there were not ghosts in such a place?

They were nearing the road when they saw, coming towards them through the late sunshine, a line of people. They were women of all ages, all on foot, although some could barely walk and limped along supported by children. Bridey and Canola quickly reined in the ponies and pulled them behind a tumble-down wall where they waited, hidden from the people on the road.

The walkers did not look up. They kept their eyes fixed on their shuffling feet, and if they raised their heads it was merely to stare for a moment at the road ahead. Bridey saw a pregnant woman stumble and fall to her knees in the mud. Another woman passed by but did not stop to help her, and the pregnant woman swore and staggered to her feet. Two children squabbled and one raised his voice in a thin wail until a slap from his mother stopped him. An old man – too old for fighting – plodded past holding the hand of the woman in front. There were no ponies. The people carried their possessions on their backs in oddly shaped bundles, or dragged them behind in small, creaking carts. Tied to the carts were a few barking dogs and one tired nanny goat.

They were the people from the abandoned farms and settlements further east, fleeing from the fighting, and from the soldiers whose savage passing had left them homeless and bereft. Bridey was numb as she watched them file past, and she felt Eadha squeeze closer, needing comfort. She patted him, unable to speak. All of Erin, it seemed, was on the move – soldiers, wounded men, and now these miserable women and children.

One of them called hoarsely, "Hurry up, we mustn't fall behind!" and her children caught up, talking soothingly and trying to hush a crying baby. Another woman shouted to a lagging boy, "Come on – or do you want to take your chances with the Tarans?"

At the mention of the Tarans the whole line hastened forward, looking back in terror, while a girl of about Bridey's age came running by, scanning the faces and calling repeatedly, "Have you seen an old man with a blue coat?" She ran on and silence fell again.

"We must be careful," whispered Canola.

"Why?"

"Because these people are as dangerous as the soldiers; they'll want our ponies."

"But . . ."

"No. We must wait till dark."

Bridey nodded slowly. She knew Canola was right. The fleeing women and children were not enemies, but they were frightened and desperate. She would be the same in their position. She considered. Why was she not running too? Why was she heading towards danger, and taking Eadha with her?

She remembered her dream – Eadha's face staring up at her from a blood-caked patch of grass.

"We *must* go on!"

It was Eadha, kicking the black pony forward, pulling at his sister. They rode off, parallel with the road but out of sight, their ponies' hoof-beats muffled on soft earth.

Evening fell and Bridey and Canola became increasingly worried. Where should they cross the road, and where was the Brugh na Ngetal? The land was flat all about, no hills in sight, nothing but brown marshes stretching into the gloom. And beyond those ... Because they were worried they began to bicker, carping at one another.

"This way now."

"Are you mad? It's right into the open."

"Well, where else, then?"

"Here – over there."

"If you want to walk right into their hands!"

"Oh, shut up."

"Fool!"

Eadha sat miserably in silence behind Bridey. He was an intruder. They didn't want him here. He knew Canola resented him and that Bridey was annoyed with him.

When Eadha felt miserable he did one of two things: he either shut his eyes and imagined how happy he could be if things were different, which made him feel pathetic and lonely, and brought on tears to relieve his feelings; or else he puffed himself up by thinking about his name. He had been enchanted to hear it in the riddle, "When Aspen, born of Willow ..."

Eadha was happy with his name. It filled him with pride just to think of it, for it was noble and historic. Eadha, the aspen, the most graceful of trees, with pale trembling leaves and delicate branches, but a heart stronger than oak. It was the aspen that provided the wood for shields, that stopped the cruelest arrow and the fastest spear. Eadha shut his eyes and was the tree, tall and slender, swaying in the wind; then he was the shield, smooth and strong and invincible. Nothing could get past him, nothing could wound him. As he rode along behind Bridey, the frightened little boy gathered his few resources – his vivid imagination and a small store of courage.

It was growing darker and still they plodded on. Mile after

mile they covered, their weariness growing. At last Eadha was asleep behind Bridey and the girl called softly to Canola:

"We've got to stop. We can't see any more, we'll get lost."

Canola turned. She could just make out the shape of the black pony and could hear the quiet jingle of his bridle.

"But look," she said and pointed ahead into the darkness.

At first Bridey could see nothing at all. There were no stars in the sky and the moon was hidden; she could just pick out the dark shadow that was Canola. Then on the horizon she saw a long mass looming above the flat earth, and she wondered how she could ever have missed it; it seemed to dominate the whole night.

It was Brugh na Ngetal, the Tomb of Reeds – the great barrow where the heroes and poets of the ancient race of Erin lay buried.

Canola dismounted and stood staring into the darkness. Around the base of the barrow were pinpricks of light – fires and torches, the lights of an army camped for the night. They gleamed and flickered, barring the way. Even if the three of them managed to cross the road, how could they hope to get safely past so many people? It was hopeless. They had come all this way to find the Tomb completely surrounded. Canola's tiredness overwhelmed her and covering her face with her hands, she collapsed to the ground.

part three

14. Brugh na ngetal

I am the hill of poets ...

Bridey woke the next morning and, rolling out of her blanket, peered sleepily from under a thornbush. They had crawled there to sleep late the night before, and she was stiff and bruised from pebbles and roots. She yawned and shook her head; it ached dully. It was as if she had been drugged, so vacant did she feel. The sky was dark, with clouds massed on the horizon, and it was late – they had slept well into the morning. Canola and Eadha were still curled up in a nest of blankets, breathing evenly.

Last night when they had seen the great barrow they had been paralysed with indecision, but at length, as the moon finally rose and shed light all about, Canola had led Bridey and Eadha towards the pale line of the road. There had been no one near. All the soldiers were gathered in the great camp at the barrow's base, and if there were lookouts posted in this direction, they saw none.

As they trotted over the road, the ponies' hooves seemed deafening on the stones, but no one galloped up to challenge them and soon they were on the edge of the marshes with the road on their left side and the army on their right. They had camped in the first cover they found, a tangle of scrub and thornbushes surrounded by marshland. With Eadha fast asleep, Bridey and Canola hastily swallowed a few mouthfuls of bread, then burrowed into the blankets and soon were sleeping deeply and dreamlessly. Now, as Bridey looked about, she saw they were nearer to Brugh na Ngetal and the army camp than they had thought. They would not have slept so soundly if they had known quite how close they lay to the soldiers.

She tightened her belt and brushed back her hair. It was tangled and coming loose, wisps floating irritatingly round her face. She was stiff and cold and miserable. It was Samain Eve, the last day of the year. What lay in store? What action would be needed, what bravery, what unknown resources? "Hopeless ..." she grimaced. "Why are we here? How ridiculous we have been."

Bridey sighed and shoved her hair away from her face. She began to crawl through the wet grass to gain a better view of the barrow. Peering through, she saw the long grassy hill rising into the sky. She saw the soldiers moving about in the camp, cooking over small fires, sharpening swords and grooming horses. She saw smoke rising in the air, and crows flapping about on the outskirts, hunting for refuse. Faint cries and the sound of hammering came to her through the cold air, a laugh trailing away, a rooster crowing, sounds of preparation and anticipation. She saw the flags with their emblem of a rearing horse, flags of Connacht. Just as Eadha had felt when the men had blundered past his hiding place, Bridey knew that nothing would induce her to look upon the soldiers in this camp as friends. Something about the war meant that friends had become as dangerous as enemies. Indeed what did 'enemy' mean when her own King was destroying the countryside and telling his subjects to die? He could talk peace with the Tarans, but he would not, because of his own desperate need for power.

Bridey watched for several minutes. The wet was seeping into the knees and elbows of her clothes, still damp from the day before. Fumbling in the pocket of her cloak, she pulled out the golden crown and placed it on her head. Cold had drained the colour from her cheeks and her lips were pale. She felt mad, and bitterly angry. Lying on her front with her chin resting on cold fists she once more contemplated the army below.

Now they looked as if they would indeed be ready for battle, and she saw the light glinting on their blades, and the bundles of spears lying ready on the ground. The laughter that reached her now was hollow, the crowing of the cockerel discordant. With the crown on her head, she was truly in control. She could send these men to their death. She could generate carnage, whip them to a frenzy and unleash them upon the enemy ... then watch them fall. A vision of a horse with arrows buried in its belly flashed through her mind; a heap of twisted bodies. She rested her face on the wet grass and pushed the crown from her head with weak fingers. She walked back to the thornbush, tucking the crown back deep into her pocket. Her legs trembled as she went.

Canola and Eadha were awake. Eadha was wolfing down his share of bread from last night, and Canola was spreading the last of the honey on a crust and telling Eadha in a subdued voice the story of a magical bee whose sting gave people the ability to create honey from marsh water. Eadha was listening spellbound and did not notice Bridey until she sat down heavily beside him. Canola stopped and Eadha cleared his throat.

"Oh," he said nervously, "how long have you been awake? What are we doing? Are we going to the Tomb?"

Bridey said nothing.

"Is there any way to get past the soldiers?" asked Canola, looking at her anxiously. "Do you think we can get through?"

"I suppose we might be able to sneak round the back," Bridey said. "It won't be easy, but we have to try." She was grim and businesslike.

They sacrificed one of Canola's blankets and tied thick wads of cloth round the ponies' feet to muffle the sound of their hooves on the stones; then Bridey began to lead the way towards Brugh na Ngetal, keeping behind the line of trees that creaked and groaned at the edge of the marshes. Now in the distance they could see the sentries, posted every hundred yards or so, leaning on spears and picking their teeth, bored and listless.

"We'll have to leave the horses," said Canola.

"No!" Bridey replied sharply. "Not yet," and Canola flushed. But Bridey was terrified of tethering the ponies and going on without them. On foot they would have no chance of escape should they be seen, and she did not like the idea of falling into the hands of the soldiers, even though they were men of Connacht.

They halted in a hollow not far from the base of the hill, less than fifty yards from Breagh's army. Crawling to the edge of the hollow they peered over. There was the Tomb of Reeds, a huge hump, the entrance blocked by a stone. They were near enough to see the white quartz glinting where it lay among the grass on the barrow's arched back, and the tall grey herm that stood at its highest point, a great stone pillar with a crudely carved face that grinned down at the men camped below. Smaller stones were ranged in a circle round the barrow's base, jutting like rotten teeth from the grass, yellow with lichen and surrounded by reeds. The doorway and lintel were decorated with sweeping spirals and jagged lightning forks. There were spirals on the standing stones too, and broad stripes and stags' antlers. Brugh na Ngetal was a place of sombre beauty, old and cold.

Canola's flesh crawled. So this was it: the Tomb of Reeds, the end of their journey. Out of nowhere she thought of her little cell at Corkaguiney, the sound of the branches moving overhead and the call of the owls. Verses of poems that she had known for years came into her head, stories of the Tuatha dé Danaan, the race of warriors and poets who had ruled Erin and built their fortress at Tara. They had made music whose echoes could still be heard if you knew how to listen, music of such sweetness that the listener became bewitched and gave up everything to follow. All her life Canola had dreamed of the Tuatha dé Danaan and had longed to hear their music, for once you heard it you were never unhappy again.

She sighed. There would be no music until Brigit's crown was given back. Turning back to the barrow she remembered the riddle, and getting heavily to her feet she fetched the beech tablet from her saddlebag.

"What's lost is found . . ." She mouthed the words, tracing the old letters with her finger. Bridey came over, relieved to be doing something, and they bent together over the tablet. Canola began to recite the last verse of the riddle.

"What's lost is found, then lost again, and found,
A Hermit and a Druid guide the way;
If Shield and Lapwing quell a maddened king,
Then peace returns before the break of day."

She smiled in triumph. It seemed a long time since she had spoken poetry, thought poetry.

Bridey met her look blankly.

"So – what does it mean?" She was numb with cold, with wet, with not knowing what to do.

Canola flushed.

"How would I know?" she retorted. "Why should I have all the answers?"

"You're the poet," Bridey muttered, "you're the one who's supposed to know, remember."

Eadha glanced anxiously from one to the other. Were they going to argue again? Quickly he said, "It's the crown – lost and found again. And you met a hermit, and Tahan gave you a map . . . and I'm a shield, because I'm Aspen, and . . . well, I don't know the rest . . . " he finished lamely. "I don't know about any kings or lapwings."

Bridey jeered, "Very good!" She was frightened: there was too much to think about. How could they find all these answers? She was tired of being responsible.

"Shall we go?" said Canola coldly. "Whatever it means we know we have to go to the Tomb. We're doing no good here. Let's just take the blessed crown and see what happens."

Bridey bit back an angry reply. It was no use getting cross with each other. She nodded.

"Yes, we can leave the ponies, as long as we make sure we've tied them properly."

"Eadha can stay with them," said Canola, "and if anyone comes along he can lead them away. Otherwise they'll just get stolen. Then where would we be?" Above all she wanted Eadha to stay behind.

"I'm not staying here!" cried Eadha. He was frightened too.

The trees were nasty looking and the call of the marsh birds was eerie and sad.

"Of course not!" exclaimed Bridey, turning to Canola. "Are you mad?"

"Are you *stupid*?" Canola hit back. "We'll surely get caught with a child tagging along."

"I'm not!"

"Quiet, you little fool!"

"Don't talk to him like that!"

Bridey glared at Canola. There was a moment of dreadful silence.

"Oh, please let me come," Eadha pleaded, holding out his hands, but he was ignored and Bridey pushed past him.

"Stay here," she snapped, and marched away. She was too angry to stay.

Canola watched her leave and stood for a few seconds trembling. She stared at Eadha, loathing him, but wanting to comfort him. Eadha snivelled. Bridey did not come back and after a few minutes Canola too stalked off and disappeared from sight. Left alone, Eadha went over to the ponies and huddled beside them. He had been left behind, after all. The trees around him began to sway and the marsh birds called again: "Hooo-ee-k! Hooo-ee-k!" Tonight was the night that the barrows opened and the Tuatha walked abroad.

Eadha thought of the Tuatha dé Danaan. How many times had he curled up near his sisters and listened to stories? His games had been about their exploits, his dreams had been full of them. Now they seemed real. The Tomb of Reeds was where they lay . . . waiting.

A tree creaked and Eadha jumped. Without thinking, he left the warmth of the ponies and within a second had scurried out of the hollow after his sister.

Bridey came back five minutes later to find Ceibhfhionn and the black pony wandering aimlessly about the hollow. She exclaimed in irritation: how could that girl leave the ponies like this? It was a miracle they had not been scared off. She caught them and tethered them securely to a bush, then waited impatiently for Canola to come back with Eadha. Where had they gone, anyway? Ten minutes later she was still waiting, but now her impatience had become acute anxiety. Where *were* they? Deciding to leave the ponies in order to search for them, she crept to the rim of the hollow and peered through the grass in the direction of the Tomb.

Between the barrow and where she stood was a wide bed of reeds. They were over a yard high and they rattled and swayed in the wind, their heavy heads nodding. In the midst of the reed bed stood a man. He had the long hair and flamboyant moustache of a warrior and his fur-lined cloak was casually flung over one shoulder as he levelled his spear.

Before him stood Canola, her face livid and her hands raised in protest. Between them both sprawled Eadha, holding his head. He had been knocked to the ground by a lazy swipe of the man's spear. Horrified, Bridey heard the man fire an order at Canola.

"Get moving," he spat, and he jabbed the air with his spear.

Canola edged towards Eadha, keeping her eyes fixed on the soldier. Leaning down she pulled at Eadha's elbow, and the boy got to his feet, whimpering and clutching at Canola's arm. Canola held him protectively and stroked his hair back from his face where a gash showed red across his forehead.

Bridey could do nothing as she saw Canola and Eadha go, Canola walking stiff and proud, Eadha stumbling by her side. She stood motionless as the warrior drove them slowly into the camp. Then they were lost in the crowd and Bridey was left alone among the reeds.

15. the eve of samain

I am the ravening boar . . .

Bridey sat, arms clasped round her knees and her teeth clenched on a fold of cloth. From time to time she lifted her eyes and scrutinised the place she had last seen Canola and her brother. Anger gusted through her, as persistent as the wind through the reeds, but hot – hot enough to make sweat break out.

She threw it away, she thought savagely, threw it all away, the fool. It's her fault! She hated her. But then Ceibhfhionn and the black pony whickered softly in her ear and her anger disappeared, leaving her shivering and guilty. She could hardly draw breath or swallow the bitter saliva that collected in her mouth as she remembered Canola's brave face. "It was *me*, I couldn't even watch my temper long enough to keep us together . . . selfish and vile . . . leaving them like that! Now they're lost!" and grinding her teeth on the rough material, she sobbed.

The thought of her mother and sisters, the Abbess, Tahan – of their grief and recriminations, made her heart beat sickly. Misery broke over her and she was completely unable to move. She abandoned herself to self-pity. She was a bad friend, a wicked sister, an ignorant, unthinking fool . . . It was the crown's fault, the ugly dented thing, with its nonsensical spirals and gouged holes where the jewels had been. None of this would have happened without the crown. Bridey could feel it digging into her hip: she wanted to get rid of it, to throw it into the marshes – but she could not. If only Canola had not gone.

Remorse was paralysing her. If she sat there long enough the sun would set and darkness would obliterate the place where Canola and Eadha had been captured. Overhead more clouds gathered, blocking out the light and creating a false dusk; bog water gleamed, lurid and glittering. At last Bridey got stiffly to her feet and began to make her way towards the camp, sloshing through puddles and catching her hair on thorns. After ten minutes of this she stopped dead in her tracks: two men were talking nearby, mumbling, bent over something lying on the ground.

"Give her a clout," said one. "That'll settle her."

There was the sound of a thump, followed by a low chuckle.

"Blast it! These teeth come right through."

Bridey craned her neck and saw on the ground between the two men a sack that moved violently and emitted a series of low grunts.

The men were soldiers – captains of the King – clad in bright colours and jewels. Slung across their shoulders each man carried a round shield, embossed with the emblem of the prancing horse, and at their sides hung long swords that clanked carelessly on the stones as they stooped.

"We'll have some fun tonight, at least!" said the first. "If Breagh insists on this suicidal action tomorrow, the least we can do is have a proper Samain."

"True," agreed his companion. "And this foolish war will be over by tomorrow evening – earlier, if the Tarans find us first. And who couldn't find us, stuck on the plain like this, beside a blasted barrow?" He snorted. "What did we do to be cursed by this idiot King?"

The other straightened up from tying the mouth of the sack and rested his hands on his hips.

"Ay, I've had enough of forced marches and ransacked hovels to last me a lifetime."

"No rich pickings here, that's for sure."

"And do you know who's been put in command of tomorrow's advance? The pretty Prince himself!"

"You jest! He could no more lead a division than draw a dagger without cutting himself . . . "

" . . . or go to bed without wetting himself!"

In her hiding place Bridey cowered as the men laughed. Something about the laughter was too loud and hearty. They walked off dragging the sack behind them.

Bridey followed at a distance, listening as they spoke in mocking tones of their companions, their servants, the mad desperation of their King. Lastly they spoke of the celebrations for Samain which were being prepared by the King's druids.

"Let's hope it's enough to strike fear into the dead."

"And the Tarans, too."

Bridey ducked low as the two men covered the last few yards and entered the camp. They greeted the other men and warmed themselves by the fire, while the other men clustered round to peer into the sack. There was more laughter.

The sky grew darker and the wind whistled across the flats. The Tomb reared into the sky and Bridey, crouched behind a bush, watched the men as they drank ale from small bronze cups and tore shreds of meat from white bones. They stoked the fires and long shadows were thrown across the uneven ground; silhouettes of men in flowing cloaks marched like giants over the grass and Bridey trembled, glancing behind her. As night fell, the dull feeling of remorse was replaced by fear as sharp and close as the long swords that hung from the belts of the warriors. The men's voices fell to a rumble, and far away on the other side of the camp someone began to sing a wild sobbing song. Sparks rose into the air and the soldiers moved together: the Eve of Samain had arrived.

Torches were being lit all over the camp and more and more voices joined in the wild singing. In the centre of the camp a cluster of makeshift huts showed where Breagh and his captains were planning the next strategy of the war. Bridey kept still and clutched nervously at Brigit's crown.

More soldiers gathered. They came from all over the camp, shouting and swearing, until at least fifty were clustered round the two men who had the sack. Some had clubs, others snub-nosed dogs snarling at the end of slim leashes. Curious, Bridey peered from behind her bush, scanning the firelit faces; then, as a man lifted up the sack and tumbled its contents onto the ground, Bridey understood.

It was a badger.

Bridey saw the pure blaze of white across the muzzle, startling in the firelight, and the soft coat, strong shoulders and broad shaggy back. The animal turned slowly this way and that, watching the soldiers: it was completely surrounded. Scenting the confused creature, the dogs strained at their leashes, desperate to be released, to bite and taste blood. Bridey clenched her teeth to stop them chattering. Her paralysis returned.

The soldiers grinned. The excitement of a badger bait: already their blood flowed faster and their thoughts dwindled to pinpricks. They forgot their kindnesses, their sympathies. The dogs were released and soon the whole world narrowed to the swing of an arm, the thump of a club, and a sense of pain and power.

Bridey buried her face in the damp grass and pressed her fists against her ears to block out the sounds, but again and again she lifted her head to watch what she couldn't bear to see. Still she heard and still she saw, and at her hip she felt the sharp edge of the crown pressing into her. Fumbling among the folds of her cloak, she clutched at it with clammy fingers, but it gave no relief, the dreadful sounds of the baiting continued. She could feel her heart thumping in her chest like a drum: *boom . . . boom . . .* and the pounding of blood in her head: *. . . boom . . . boom . . . boom . . .* Minutes passed slowly and the excitement faded. The baiting degenerated into a slow wearisome battle, its ending longed for and dreaded.

In the circle of men, the badger was held down and finished off. The dogs were dragged away. "Poor old Brock!" One of the soldiers laughed. The dogs cringed and licked their wounds, and the men dispersed.

Bridey's stupor had passed. She crouched behind the bush, and peering through the twigs at the blood and trampled grass, she felt a calm powerful rage. What she had seen had terrified her: the men had showed her the extent of their violence. She remembered the crown, the screams of the dying, the longing to lacerate and destroy; then she remembered the strolling badgers of the oak-wood. Shrugging off her darker thoughts she focused singlemindedly on what she had to do. She knew it was madness to venture into the camp. It would be simple for any of the men to spot her, and she pictured herself caught, surrounded by braying men. But the likelihood of capture only spurred her on. Her anger was like a bright shield held in front of her, and she got to her feet and began to walk slowly and carefully into the camp. She kept to the shadows, avoiding the torches and fires, hiding behind the fragile huts and lines of stamping horses. She was right in the middle of the camp when shouts and cheering caused her to stop and look towards the entrance of the Tomb.

A dozen men were hauling the great rock from the door. They heaved and grunted as the ponderous boulder shifted slowly, then, with a final rush it trundled a few yards down the slope and came to rest with a thump and a sigh of crushed reeds. The soldiers cheered, gazing at the jagged hole of the entrance. Torches were shaken in triumph, but no light penetrated the darkness of Brugh na Ngetal. It crouched, huge and humped, mouth open.

Bridey felt taut. Like Canola she was tall and strong and brave. She must find her. She must find Eadha. Keeping to the shadow of a row of chariots, she walked right into the heart of Breagh's camp.

16. the Battle song

I am the roaring winter sea ...

Canola was alone in the King's hut, standing stiffly with her hands tied behind her back. Her feet were tied too, but loosely, so she was able to shuffle cautiously to the door and peer outside. She groaned from the pain in her head as she moved; there was a band of steel at her temples. The little hut was heavily guarded, with soldiers on either side of the door, and nearby a group of men were playing dice, their swords ready beside them. Canola shuffled back, suddenly dizzy. She had been left alone, or as good as alone, for Eadha was shocked and silent, staring in front of him, his face caked in dried blood.

Underfoot the grass was yellow from loss of sun, dry and trampled. On the rough wicker walls hung weapons and shields, and a large scroll of parchment covered with the ciphers of the druids. A table had been fashioned from planks and upon it stood an inkhorn, a quill and many scraps and crumpled balls of vellum, the discarded strategies of Breagh and his men. Propped in the corner was an assortment of whips and lashes with which the King's captains had extracted information from captured Tarans. The severed heads of these prisoners now gruesomely adorned the external walls of the hut, while others had been thrust on spikes and set at the entrance of the camp as a warning. Canola tried to forget them, but they haunted her, floating through her mind, disembodied and staring.

Despite her terror and the banging in her head, she herself was unhurt. No one had dared lay a finger on her, for she had kept them at bay with all the verse she could muster, inspired to new heights by an overwhelming fear of being hurt. Eadha, however, had not been so lucky. When questioned by the bloated Captain of the Guard, he had answered innocently, stammering, and had been rewarded by a punch that brought the blood pouring from his nose. Since then he had sat silent and petrified in the corner, trussed up like a chicken and forgotten by the soldiers.

When they had been brought to the King's hut by the sentry who had found them, Canola had not been tongue-tied for long. No, she had answered scathingly, she was not a spy. How shortsighted must a King have become if he cannot tell a loyal subject from a traitor? Did she look like a Taran?

King Breagh was seated at the table, his hands spread in front of him. Canola gazed at them. They were large and pale and knotted with thick veins of a delicate blue. The fingernails of one hand were immaculate, with several rings gleaming above the knuckles; but the nails of the other were chewed to the quick and the sides bitten till they bled. From time to time Breagh played with a large silver brooch that lay on the table before him.

To one side of the King stood the bulky Captain of the Guard, to the other a druid who reminded Canola of the mad hermit they had met by the river – gaunt and humourless. But this man did not burn feverishly like the anchorite; instead he regarded Canola with cold, round eyes. The King listened to Canola and raised an eyebrow, and the questions had followed thick and fast. Canola had lied desperately, wittily, keeping in her mind all the time the face of Liadan, the poet who never trembled, or stumbled on a rhyme.

"Oh, for pity's sake, my lord," she scoffed, "can you not spot one of your own bards? Call for Liadan and she will vouch for me."

"I have dispensed with the Corkaguiney hen-wife," drawled the King, and he watched closely for Canola's reaction. She did not falter.

"She was too sharp for your dull wits, no doubt. Do you dispense with all your advisers so readily? Perhaps you should get rid of this skinny magician," and she nodded at the druid, "or your great dancing bear, here," and she winked at the Captain of the Guard. Breagh snorted and looked at her with a glimmer of interest.

Canola quaked, but she knew that insolence was her only hope. If she could convince them she was a true poet, then at least they would think twice about killing her. But her courage wavered at the thought of Liadan – had Breagh truly got rid of her? If he dared defy the greatest bard in Connacht, he would not fear swatting an upstart like herself. The questions continued, some drawled by the King, others barked by the druid.

"Tell me your name."

"And your origins."

"What are you doing here?"

"And who is this child?"

"You dress like a poet, but act like a spy. Explain yourself, girl, and without the fancy riddles."

During a silence, the druid bent and whispered in the King's ear, his eyes never leaving Canola for a second. She saw a shadow pass across Breagh's face and he leaned back in his chair, eyes gleaming.

Breagh was a big man, with a sharp attractive face and long black hair. Not yet thirty, he was already King of Connacht and Commander of the biggest force to be mustered in living memory. All through his childhood he had dreamed of exerting power over others; his daydreams had been fed by poets who sang of victory, and at night he had lain awake and planned sweet revenge on all those who had slighted him. For weakness was what Breagh most despised, and he saw it everywhere: in those without power; in those without wealth. He looked with distaste at Eadha and hated him for his snivelling and for his bloody nose. He hated the girl too, for the unnatural colour of her hair. He no longer feared poets: he was now so strong that no words could hurt him. He had the power to crush anyone who defied him, poet or otherwise. But when the tall druid stooped again to whisper, Breagh felt a thrill of fear.

"Remember Spiral Castle . . ." came the soft words, and the

King gnawed nervously at the side of his thumb. He knew well that Samain Eve was traditionally perilous: on this night kingdoms were invaded, rulers overthrown, despots destroyed ... "Remember Brugh na Ngetal, my lord. The gods are hungry." Kings died on Samain Eve, the last night of the year; were slain and laid to rest in the cold barrows, the cold spiral castles.

Breagh looked from the druid to the Captain of the Guard. Always advice was conflicting; better to trust to his own instincts. Breagh found it difficult to trust anyone at all. The druids were treacherous, loyal only to themselves. The Guard remained loyal, but only as long as the coffers were full, and the gold coins were disappearing fast.

Breagh gnawed again at his thumb. After months of war, reality had become hazy. He no longer saw the discontent of his soldiers, or heard their mutinous talk. He was oblivious to the hundreds of dead left unburied after each engagement, and he had lost sight of the fact that the farmers who did his fighting for him were more worried about their ruined harvest than about the fight for supremacy in the bleak marshes of the border country. The King knew he was hated by many, but a myth surrounded and protected him.

The Captain of the Guard stepped forward.

"We must take care, my lord," he said. "The Eve of Samain is no time for hasty judgements. The mouth of the Tomb is open and who knows what beings are abroad. Keep the girl under guard, my lord, and we need fear neither her, nor the spirits." He cast a nervous look at Canola. "We cannot harm a poet – least of all tonight."

The King raised an eyebrow and turned to the druid.

"Well?" he said. "What do you suggest? Should I be alarmed by another gabbling bard?"

"Assuredly not, my lord," said the druid. "The Captain reads it wrong. There is powerful magic at our disposal tonight, and this girl is a mystery, perhaps a danger. She says she is of Corkaguiney, yet what is that straw-coloured stuff doing on the head of one of our women? She is a bloodless thing, not one of us. What better offering shall we find to pacify the gods and further our cause?"

The captain was shaking his head in agitation.

"I beg you, sire, do not listen. How rashly have these druids advised you thus far? What foolishness would this be? Kill the other prisoners, by all means, but spare the poet. The very Tuatha themselves would be angered by such a sacrifice. We cannot kill a poet upon the Tomb of Reeds. It is blasphemy, and we do not need any more bad luck. We are already fighting with old men and children. We need good magic, not this madness! We have lost too many men."

Breagh laughed gratingly.

"Men! A few thousand labourers! We have plenty more of those. I shall not be stopped by such talk of economy. This girl would burn well. I like the idea."

The druid smiled in triumph, and the Captain shrugged.

"Very well, my lord," he said. "I shall issue the order for tomorrow's attack. We advance at dawn." As he walked out, Canola saw the expression of disbelief on his face.

Breagh leaned back in his chair and rubbed his eyes. He was tired, but he smiled at the thought of the Samain fires. He was not frightened, he told himself, by all this talk of ghosts. He would burn prisoners and make his own magic. He could not lose, not now.

They left Canola in the heavily guarded hut while Breagh inspected his horse-soldiers and the druids supervised the final preparations for Samain. It was dark outside and they had left only a guttering candle to light the interior of the hut. Canola was thirsty, and it was hard for her to concentrate on anything while her tongue felt like a piece of leather in her mouth. She had lost all hope.

Eadha began to whimper and she tried to comfort him, but was unable to make his dazed eyes focus on her face. At last she sat down beside him and huddled close.

"I want Bridey," the boy whispered at last.

"Yes, so do I."

"Where is she?"

"I don't know."

"Is she dead?"

"N-no . . . of course not."

She patted Eadha's hands and stroked his cheek. She wanted to kiss him, to make him feel better, but it was no good. Oh, why had she lost Bridey? She wanted her so badly. How had they ever argued? She vowed never to argue again.

But it was all over. It was only a matter of time before they were dragged out and murdered; she wondered whether they would adorn the walls of the King's hut. Desperate with thirst, she moved closer to Eadha and sobbed drily. The candle flickered and died and they were left in total darkness. Soon Canola's head drooped and she fell into a delirious sleep.

She was woken by a burst of light and noise as Breagh and his captains came back into the hut. They did not seem to see her as they set torches in the stands and brought chairs and a cask of wine. The table was swept free of maps, and platters of food were set upon it; a smell of warm fat filled the air.

Breagh was in good spirits and his eyes glittered like the flickering torches. His captains, resplendent in their cloaks and jewels, were drunk and reckless. One of the men saw her and bent down to look. She felt the hot sour breath on her face.

"What's this, then? A lady in the King's quarters?"

Breagh frowned, unamused.

"A spy," he snapped, "with some Taran waif. She calls herself a poet and has scared the daylights out of your fat Captain."

Everyone laughed and Canola was pulled roughly to her feet.

"Give us a song, girl," they cried.

"Ay, a little music. Fetch her a stool."

She was forced up in the midst of the drunken soldiers. They prodded and pushed her, calling for her to sing.

"Give us a ballad!"

"Or a love-song, you pretty sparrow."

"Not a sparrow, you clod, a nightingale, a nightingale!"

Faces leered and swam as Canola bent her head and fixed her

eyes on the floor. The pain in her head was getting worse all the time. Her face burned, and again and again she licked her dry lips, until someone thrust a cup at her and she swallowed some wine. But it only left her more thirsty than before, and when she tried to sing her voice cracked and she fell silent amid the jeering. Her thoughts went to her little harp, tucked safe at the bottom of Ceibhfhionn's saddlebag. Thoughts of her harp led to thoughts of Bridey, and she broke down and wept.

"Oh, get away then, girl," cried Breagh in vexation, hating the sight of her pale hair and her tears, and he pulled her off the stool and pushed her back into the corner with Eadha. "Fetch a real poet!"

One of the captains ran from the hut and five minutes later a bard stood before them. He ran his fingers over the strings of his harp and, smiling at the drunken men, he began to play. Despite her misery, Canola lifted her head in admiration: truly he had skill that would charm the fish from the water and the heart from a lover's breast. Closing her eyes she leaned her aching head against the wall and listened.

It was a song of heroism and war, of warriors noble and strong, who trampled their enemies beneath thundering chariot wheels with no mercy. The words made the hair rise at the back of her neck and beside her she felt Eadha stir and look up at the man with the harp. The boy's eyes lost their dazed expression and became wistful and happy. In the song the hero donned his fox-furred cloak. His lady-love lifted pure white hands to caress his face, and she pinned a sprig of rowan to his sleeve. As he rode away the echo of the horns followed him into battle, and when he fought the foe fled screaming, cowardly faces pale with fear. They fell into pits and died upon stakes; they were pierced by burning arrows and died in flames; they died screaming, sliced in two by the hero's sword.

As Canola listened her memories of the battlefield with its stinking corpses and hopping crows began to fade, and although she struggled to remember what was real, the words were too powerful. The little hut was stuffy and smelled of sweat and wine, but lovely pictures swam before her eyes as in the song the battle reached its climax and was over. The harp became melodious and soothing. There was no need to think any more, no need to worry. What does it matter anyway? It is Samain, the beginning of the darkest part of the year: winter, with hungry mouths and sickness and crying babies. But in the spring the grass will grow again and cover the battlefields. Besides, what can anyone possibly do to stop it? Canola could not even keep her eyes open. This time tomorrow, she thought, I will be dead. And the words are beautiful . . . it is like being rocked in the gentle sea . . . the gentle . . . sea . . .

17. PRINCE LÍR

I am the wave that returns to the shore ...

There was one young man in the stuffy hut who did not find the words of the bard so stirring, but instead felt them break over him with a wintry bleakness. It was the young man who stood near the door, hands thrust deep in his pockets and one eye twitching nervously. His appearance outshone even that of the King's captains. He had a beautiful face and quantities of thick black hair caught up in plaits and thongs that glinted here and there with gems. He was extremely graceful, and beside him the King and his men looked clumsy – they were drunken and flushed, he was cool and proud, staring scornfully at the bard and the soldiers. It was not hard for him to look aloof; he despised them. They were grotesque, and the song was a lie. Young Prince Lir clenched his hands more tightly in his pockets and wished he did not feel so completely alone.

He was a prince in name only, and even his name was not his own, for it had been given him by the King, who said it suited him better. Breagh often gave Lir things the boy didn't want – gold, jewellery, a goshawk and a nervous, half-trained horse. The King had nothing to offer that Lir truly wanted, and the boy lived in a miserable state of confusion and homesickness.

He had been living in Killala in the far north, receiving his education in the traditional manner from a community of priests and scholars. The King's court had passed through, and Breagh, taking a fancy to the solemn student, had commanded Lir to accompany him to Cruachan. Lir had been keen to obey. Who would not hero-worship such a powerful and hawk-faced King?

149

Life at court was very different to life as a scholar. Since Midsummer, Lir had spent his time in running errands, listening to flattery and court gossip, and learning how to fight with a sword. It was glittering and exciting at first, full of music and feasting, but of late it had become grim, bloodthirsty and monotonous. In the beginning Lir had been dazzled by the splendid captains, with their weapons and their elaborate oiled hair. He had been spoiled with gifts, pampered and indulged by all those who sought the approval of the King. It had been like a game: dressing in rich fabrics and furs, using precious fragrances, hanging gold and jewels around his neck . . . Breagh had petted him like a dog and given him power, and it was strange for Lir to have men twice his age duck their heads and look at him with fear. He copied the King's arrogance, but in reality it was he who was afraid of these men, the professional soldiers, with their vicious speech and hatred of inferiors. In time he also learnt to hate the man who had plucked him from his familiar scholastic community.

For Breagh was never truly kind. He treated Lir like a plaything, a doll to be picked up and discarded according to whim. At first he had been amused by Lir; it had been entertaining to give him power and to set him against other court favourites. But now the war took all Breagh's time and Lir found himself forgotten, or used merely as errand boy and ornament. Now there was nothing but battles, horrendous defeats and the inevitable execution of prisoners of war. He longed to escape, but did not dare to attempt it.

Lir had been sickened by the wastefulness of the war, and now he was frightened by the position of authority into which, as favourite of the King, he had been thrust. He had made no friends, only enemies; sometimes he thought he would drown in his homesickness. But he could not go home – he was not wanted there. The parents who had sent him away to receive his schooling would not want him back. Lir missed his teachers and the mountains of Killala. He had been bored there, but now he longed to be stuck on a hard bench in the main hall, learning etiquette, Latin or the way to train falcons.

Lir had looked forward to his first battle. As a boy he had been given a bow and told to hunt, been given a wooden sword and told to play. Who would not long for their first battle? He was a prince, now, so he would not even have to slog in the mud with the common foot-soldiers, but could ride on a roan mare at the head of a hundred men; he could use them just as he had used wooden soldiers as a child. He would not care about the men he fought and killed because he would be up above them, and they would be on the ground in the mud. How he had longed to fight. He had listened to Breagh and his captains and had imagined sticking a spear into another man: it would be good sport, just like hunting.

But his first battle had been spent lying in a ditch with a dying mule crushing his legs, and all he remembered was the rusty taste of blood in his mouth and the sound of the mule coughing. Breagh's captains had pulled him out and slapped him on the back, laughing at the sight of the boy's terror and confusion. Since then, despite numerous battles, each with greater casualties than the last, Lir had not become accustomed to the horror and screaming; he had never grown to love it as he thought he would. Nothing was as he imagined. It was all disgusting and pointless.

With a twang, the bard finished his ballad and the soldiers applauded, telling each other how they would run the Tarans into the sea. No one spoke of defeat, and wineskins were passed round again. As the door banged, Lir was pushed to one side and a hush fell in the crowded hut as the men looked to see who had entered. It was the tall druid, flanked by four others, white robes gleaming. The captains stared, a few muttered to their neighbours; the priests were hated by the soldiers, who feared their magic. The druids grinned back. They despised the captains as crude, drunken killers.

"I have come for the girl," their leader declared, and he turned his fishy eyes towards Canola where she cringed in the corner. "The ceremonies begin within the hour . . . we have sharpened our knives."

The King smiled.

"We will attend you with due solemnity," he said. Lir looked curiously at the strange young woman whose colourless hair was tangled about her face. She lifted her chin and her voice croaked slightly as she spoke.

"My friend," – she bowed to the bard – "you have nimble fingers. I hope you fare better than most of the court poets."

She was dragged to the door but was stopped by the bard, who put a hand on her arm and spoke in a strange voice.

"If you are of Liadan, give us a small sample of the great bard's verse. Please, from one poet to another." Canola stared at him blankly.

"I am tired of songs," she said.

The man frowned.

"Did my singing displease you? Why will you not let me hear the sweetness of your voice?"

"You are a powerful rhymer," Canola replied, "but do you truly think this is a time for songs of war? Are you a musician or a mere mouthpiece? Do you simply sing on command? Can poets be bought so easily by kings?"

The man stared at her with dislike.

"What right have you to tell me of my conscience?" he demanded. "I do not see *you* prospering, for all your good intentions."

Breagh tipped some more wine down his throat and said listlessly, "Will someone please take the girl?"

The druid stepped forward with a strip of white cloth, and the men were surprised at the violence of Canola's struggles.

"I will not be ... silent! You cannot ... " But the gag was between her teeth. Eadha tried to get to her, but the soldiers held him back.

Breagh fiddled with the silver brooch at his throat. He glanced at Eadha.

"You, Lir, take this whelp and put him with the other prisoners. Tell the guard that I want the prisoners brought to the Tomb. The fires will soon be lit. Druid, take the girl. I'm tired of these ranting poets."

As Canola was bundled through the door by the druids, Lir

stared into her furious green eyes with a strange sense of
recognition. Her face was in some way familiar, although he
was certain he could never have seen her before. He wanted to
follow, to speak to her, but Breagh was issuing orders and Lir
had not yet learned how to disobey. Grabbing Eadha by the
shoulder, he sliced through his bonds and with the child
stumbling and snivelling behind him, he went outside, grateful
to be away from the heat and smell of the hut.

The Taran prisoners stood huddled in a long wicker cage at the
other end of the camp. They stared quietly through the bars,
and Lir looked back, trying not to hate them, for they were a
pitiful sight with their matted beards and rags. Torches stood
at each corner of the cage, lighting their hungry faces, and a
clanking could be heard above the rattling of the reeds.

"What's that noise?" asked Eadha, glancing round. He was
afraid – it was Samain Eve, there were witches.

"Look," the Prince pointed to the men in the cage, and
Eadha saw that round the neck of every man was a heavy metal
collar, and through each collar ran a clumsy chain. The men
held the chain to relieve their necks of some of its weight.

Lir greeted the guards.

"Give me the keys," he commanded, "and go to the Tomb.
Replacements are on their way and you are needed by the
Captain. Hurry!"

The guards recognised the Prince and sneered, but without
questioning his orders they collected their weapons and began
to trudge off towards the entrance of the Tomb where the
Samain fires had begun to blaze. Lir trembled slightly. He had
lied. No replacements were coming, and he was alone with the
Taran prisoners. An idea was forming in his head and it made
him shiver.

Beside him, Eadha was restless. Away from the King's hut
he was feeling better, despite the throbbing of his battered
face. This person did not frighten him. Lir looked like a prince
from the old fables.

"Who are you? What's your name? Are you a Taran?" He

pulled at Lir's cloak, half-curious, half-agitated, touching the Prince's hand. He was confused; he assumed he was in the enemy camp. He was certain Lir could not be of Connacht – he was too exotic. "Are you a Taran? Have you seen my sister? She must be here. Will you help me look? What's happened to Canola?" He had forgotten how he came to be here. All he knew was that he must find Bridey.

Lir looked down.

"Who's Canola? Is she the poet? Is she your sister?"

"No, Bridey's my sister. Canola's her friend. It's Bridey who's ... " – he decided to trust Lir, he had no option – " ... who's got the crown." But the Prince pushed past him and looked back at the prisoners.

"The crown," repeated Eadha. "Like the riddle says: 'What's lost is found, then lost again, and found ...' My sister's got Brigit's crown."

Lir looked down again.

"Are you a poet too?"

"No," hissed the boy in exasperation, "I'm not the poet, I'm the shield. Eadha. What's your name?" He peered at the Prince intently.

Without thinking, Lir muttered, "They used to call me *Aidhircléog*, Lapwing. What of it? It's a stupid name." He remembered how Breagh had laughed. Instead of laughing, Eadha gave a sigh of relief.

"Lapwing!" he said, and he leaned against the Prince.

Lir frowned. What was this nonsense? Again he stared fixedly at the men in the cage, remembering the young poet's defiance in the King's hut and the way she had refused to go quietly. He had never seen anyone stand up to Breagh before, and the girl's behaviour had planted a seed in his own compliant mind. Besides, her face gave him disturbing thoughts ... the strange colour of her hair.

He had seen what happened to prisoners, many times. He had watched the slaughter time and again, and each time he had felt as if some part of him was being carved out and thrown away, leaving emptiness. He looked at the caged men and thought of their heads stuck on sticks. He walked up to the cage and looked at the man nearest him, and the man looked back with an expression of tired hatred. Lir held out his hand and gave the man the keys to the chains and to the cage. They jangled faintly as they brushed the stout wicker bars. The man looked at him mistrustfully.

"You can go free," said the Prince. "Run fast – your army lies due east. It's a matter of five miles."

"It's a trick," said the prisoner and he thrust the keys back.

"No, it's . . ." Lir hesitated, then once again he threw the keys through the bars. They fell at the man's feet. Turning, Lir grabbed Eadha's arm and began to walk quickly towards the entrance of the Tomb. In mute astonishment the Taran prisoners watched him go.

The entrance of the Tomb was lit by fires on either side. There were fires on the hillside too, and men could be seen tending them as Lir and Eadha hurried through the camp. Everywhere men were drinking and celebrating. Samain songs rose into the air and, as he listened, Eadha remembered the Samain holidays in his own home – the races and dancing, the roast pork with apples . . . It had been nicer there. They carried on, Eadha stumbling as he tried to keep up. No one challenged them and they went on until they stood at the foot of the great hill.

Eadha thought that Lir was taking him to Canola. Perhaps he knew where Bridey was too.

"Is your father a king?" he asked.

Prince Lir walked on. The tic had once more begun to twitch his eyelid. After a moment Eadha pulled at his sleeve.

"Is your father a king?" he repeated.

Lir looked straight ahead.

"No, not a king," he said, "and I'm not a real prince, either. Anyway, it doesn't matter, my father's probably dead." This little boy's questions puzzled him. No one had ever asked about his family. It pleased him to think that his father might be dead. He could easily have been killed in battle. He missed his father less when he thought he might be dead. His mind was full of memories: the elder brother he had played with; the mother whose face was both kindly and distant; the little fair-haired baby sister ... But he did not seem to be able to remember what his father looked like. He could picture his mouth, laughing, with white teeth – but nothing more. If he tried to remember the whole man he simply got a vision of someone in furs, stiff and formal.

Eadha contemplated the Prince and wondered what to do. The riddle seemed to be coming true. Perhaps Bridey had found Canola by now; perhaps Canola had escaped. He looked at the crowd of men celebrating in front of Brugh na Ngetal. Certain that he would be able to find his sister somewhere in the crowd, he began pulling Lir along behind him. Lir followed submissively, deep in thought.

They went among the crowd where the air was thick with the smell of wine. Men were frenzied, losing themselves in the noise, the swaying lights, the rhythmic drums of the druids. At the sight of the druids Lir pulled himself together. Breagh would be waiting for his prisoners and they must be careful. Pulling his cloak over his face, he began to make his way through the reeds at the base of the barrow, pretending to stagger like a drunken man. Soon he and Eadha were hidden in a clump of tall grass a few yards below the entrance, in the shadow of the huge rock that earlier had barred the door. Peering out, Lir saw the gaunt druid and his followers, resplendent in their white robes, and he ducked back, heart beating fast.

In the firelit entrance of the Tomb, Breagh stood motionless, his face grim, staring into the darkness. Where were the prisoners? He needed their blood for Samain magic. The wine was making his head spin and the heat of the fires had beaded his face with sweat. He wiped his forehead and smiled. He knew about the power of blood. Human sacrifice allows a man to woo the gods. It captures the force that rules the stones. It gives great power. Where were his prisoners?

Glancing behind him he saw Canola standing in the shadows of the Tomb entrance. She had been untied and her gag removed. He was reassured: one poet was worth a hundred foot-soldiers. Only he would have the courage to tamper with the life of a bard, for it was taboo to harm a poet. His eyes gleamed. He was not afraid. Tomorrow, with his powers renewed, he would defeat the Tarans. Niall of Tara would grovel before him, and he, Breagh, would be High King of all Erin.

Canola saw the King watching her. Everything was like a dream – the fires, the singing of the soldiers, the whirling dance of the druids . . . Then torchlight glanced off Breagh's sword and Canola was jolted back to her senses; her legs turned to jelly and threatened to give way; fear washed over her and sweat trickled down the back of her legs. She wanted Bridey, she wanted Liadan, she wanted . . . at the thought of her mother she began to cry helplessly. Her headache was still like an iron band around her head, tighter and tighter . . . The King was calling for his prisoners; the Captain of the Guard was protesting, the druids gesticulating. She shut her eyes for an instant, and when she opened them again, Breagh loomed over her.

"Well, poet," he said, "it seems for the moment that you will have to die alone. The men want some entertainment." He grabbed her by the shoulders and snarled, "You have jinxed us after all. Where are my prisoners?"

Canola struggled to draw breath as Breagh's face swam before her eyes.

"I – I won't die alone," she managed to say. "It is you who are alone, Breagh, can't you see . . ." Her voice failed and she fell to the ground with the King standing over her, looking as if he would kick her for speaking the truth. Behind him a druid paused in his dancing to watch, silhouetted against the light of the fires, and in the camp below the crowd milled and seethed. Breagh turned and brushed past the druid as Canola sobbed, wondering if this white-robed figure had come to take her to her death.

Canola . . .

In the distance she heard her name called. Whose voice

could it be? Her mind was playing tricks. She remembered a dream of a tall stone in a clearing; St. Brigit calling her name.

"Canola!"

A druid was hissing, hood drawn slightly back. Canola blinked. Two green eyes looked out from beneath the hood, and Canola saw black hair and a pointed chin. She put out her hand to grab the hem of the white robe, and the druid bent down and clasped her with a warm hand.

It was Bridey.

18. tuatha dé danaan

... and only I know the secret of the Tomb.

When Bridey left the scene of the badger baiting to look for Canola she had been driven by a reckless bravery that lasted long enough to take her into the middle of the camp, but deserted her completely at the sight of so many armed men and so much drunkenness. She was amazed that she was not spotted as she kept her head down and darted from one patch of shadow to another. At one point her way was barred by a group of men who were noisily attempting to right an upturned chariot, and she ducked behind a pyramid of barrels and peered out.

"Put your backs into it!" cried the soldier in charge of the operation. The men grumbled and muttered.

"Listen to him, the windbag."

"Ay, quick with his gob, but slow to get his hands dirty."

"Soft as babies, these captains!"

They chuckled and heaved, while behind them another horseman cantered up and hailed them.

"Do any of you know where the bard is hiding? The damned fellow's nowhere to be found, and the King is calling for his pretty voice."

The captain who was supervising the righting of the chariot laughed sympathetically.

"You'd better find him then, and quick," he said, and scratched his chin. "I thought I saw him a minute since, talking with the drummers, yonder," and he pointed towards a cluster of small fires nearby.

The second captain called his thanks as he galloped away,

spattering the men with mud. They swore beneath their breath, looking bitterly at the King's man – safe on horseback.

"What does Breagh need with another poet?" scoffed one to his neighbour. "They say he's got one already – a Taran woman. Caught her spying in the marshes. White hair, like a swan."

"Yellow," contradicted his friend, "yellow as buttercups."

"Get on there!" called the captain, and they fell silent and pushed against the heavy chariot.

Bridey knelt quaking behind the barrels. So, Canola was with the King. But where was the King, and how could she get there? Would Eadha be there too? Glancing to left and right, she began to walk quickly towards the centre of the camp where a cluster of low buildings crouched in the mud and, drawing close, she saw the heavy flag of Connacht flapping sluggishly above the nearest hut. It was surrounded on all sides by guards and she swallowed in horror at the grisly trophies that adorned it. This must be the King's. Unconsciously she ran her eye over the wicker walls: shoddy work, they would not withstand even a gentle storm. They were obviously temporary affairs, easily erected and as easily dismantled. She saw the captain ride up and dismount. Behind him came a man with a harp, and there was a flurry of activity as he was hustled into the hut. The guards clustered round to see what was happening and to catch a glimpse of the white-haired captive inside. Bridey took advantage of the excitement and dodged round the men until she was standing in the narrow gap that separated the King's hut and the hut adjoining it. She stayed completely still, hardly daring to breathe, hoping desperately that the guards would not come too close. For a moment she was deafened by her own breathing, but gradually, as she listened, she was able to distinguish voices coming to her through the gaps in the wall. At length one voice only could be heard – the voice of the man with the harp; and for a moment, as Bridey studied the battered wicker of the King's hut, the music took her back and she remembered how her mother would sing as she taught her daughters to weave. Bridey, the youngest, would laugh and clap her hands, while her sisters bent their heads studiously over slippery fronds of willow. Now as she leant her head against the wall, soothed by the memory of her family, she realised with a jolt that the chinks in the wicker – amateurish and loosely woven – afforded a clear view of the interior. Squinting through she was able to make out the people within.

In the centre of the crowded room stood the bard, strumming on his harp and singing a valiant song of war. Craning her neck, Bridey tried to see into the dark corners of the room. Nothing, only the listening captains and a handsome young man lounging by the door. Then, as she peered down, she saw slumped on the floor the huddled shape of Canola; next to her, bound with thick ropes, was Eadha.

Bridey had not realised how frightened she was of these men until she saw her friend in their midst, and for a moment she was completely at a loss, but then a sound behind her made her turn and look through the tiny slits into the adjoining hut. It was empty, but she was just in time to see a white figure disappearing through the low door. A solitary candle stood upon a table, shedding a feeble light by which she could make out a jumble of pale linen and a few branches of oak, the autumn leaves dry and brown.

A burst of applause came from the King's hut, hooting calls and cheering, and pulling out her little knife Bridey began to slice and hack at the wall of the empty hut, knowing that any noise she made would be drowned by the uproar next door. Her knife was sharp, but the wicker was tough, and Bridey had only made a small gap before the noise began to die down. Stooping, she pushed herself through the gap, wriggling and kicking. She thought her hair would be torn from her head and her cloak from her back as with a rush she tumbled head first into the dark hut of the druids and lay for a moment, panting softly in the silence, a deep scratch on her cheek and another on her calf. Behind her in the King's hut she could hear voices, and she was sure one of them was that of Canola – slightly shrill, but brave. Bridey became dizzy at the sound, she wanted to run to Canola, regardless of the danger. She needed her . . .

they should be together. Looking about, she contemplated what to do.

The pile of linen turned out to be the long white robes worn by the druids on sacred occasions. They lay discarded on the table amid a clutter of candle ends, acorns and frayed pieces of rope, and as Bridey dabbed at her cheek with her cloak, she suddenly remembered the words of the hermit by the river – could it only have been yesterday? It seemed weeks ago. She sighed; if only she and Canola had not been separated, if only they had not argued; if only . . . She heard again the words of the hermit and saw his eyes burning with a strange light: "The world is one soul, with no division. Take white garments to hide yourselves . . . white robes dipped in blood . . ."

Here were the robes. Maybe now she could go unnoticed right to the very entrance of Brugh na Ngetal. Then . . . what was the last piece of rhyme that Canola had recited? Bridey could not remember any of it. Something about . . . lost and found, and lost . . . As she pulled one of the creased white robes over her head, she wished she was taller. She had seen a group of druids as she dodged through the camp and they had seemed vast, looming like ghosts over the dark ground, their hands clenched round blazing torches. There were no torches in the hut but Bridey's eyes were caught by a little drum, and she slung it round her neck and gave it a gentle tap. It resounded hollowly . . . *clock, clock* . . . fleetingly Bridey remembered Tahan's old face. I wish I'd been kinder to him, she thought.

A scream came from the King's hut and Bridey froze. It was Canola, angry, or in pain. Pulling the white hood over her face, Bridey grabbed a second robe and left the druid's hut in time to see Canola being dragged struggling away by a group of the white-robed men.

She followed them closely, no longer keeping to the shadows, walking on tiptoes and tapping the drum, swaying from side to side in imitation of a sacred trance. Scarcely daring to look up, she sensed rather than saw Canola's clumsy, stumbling progress, as she was pulled along by two tall druids with hands like pincers. When they reached the entrance the druids began to hoot and wail, beating their drums and tearing their hair in a frenzy; the flames leaped into the darkness and, in the camp below, the soldiers began to clap and cheer. Bridey took a deep breath and started to whirl slowly, keeping an eye on the gaping door of the Tomb. In the shadow of the heavy lintel stood Canola, looking blankly in front of her, her fair hair dishevelled and her face pinched and pale.

Bridey tapped on her drum and edged closer. She saw the King approach and speak to Canola, his face haughty and cruel. Canola replied, her green eyes wide and angry; then her legs gave way and she crumpled at Breagh's feet. For a moment Bridey thought Breagh would kill Canola. His face was open, his expression unguarded, and he looked at the poet as if she was the focus of all his fear and hatred. But then with a sneer he turned away, and Bridey felt a jolt as he brushed past her, knocking her elbow. Her heart was in her mouth as she moved forward and put out her hand, hissing at Canola to attract her attention.

Please look up, please . . .

As their hands met both girls felt a wave of love and relief. Bridey gave a choking laugh, and squeezing Canola's fingers she murmured, "Don't worry . . ." but then the tall druid loomed over them and she dropped Canola's hand in terror.

"Do not be hasty, brother," he said. "She is *ours*, never fear," and Bridey jumped back and spun away, her heart pounding, desperate at leaving Canola. But the druid suspected nothing and he peered down at the poet and rubbed his cold hands.

The dancing continued, the beat of the drums grew louder, and from down in the camp came the braying of war-horns and the squealing of the pipes. Bridey beat on her drum and felt sweat begin to trickle down her chest and sides. To her left, a druid was tipping back a wooden bowl and drinking deeply. When he lowered the bowl his lips were red with blood and his eyes gleamed as he passed the bowl to his neighbour.

"Drink, brother," he said.

At last the bowl came to Bridey, and she felt eyes turn upon

163

her. She knew the offering must be accepted and, sickened, she held out her hands to take the bowl. But it was heavy and the smooth wood was slippery, and Bridey, fumbling desperately, slopped its gory contents down the white of her robe. She was drenched in blood and the bowl clattered on the stone and rolled away. Bridey looked at her hands, smeared with red, dark lines round the nails ... she remembered a sword, her arm slashing down, the screams of the dying.

The druids stared and for a moment there was silence, but a loud laugh roused them and they turned to see Breagh pointing mockingly at the clumsy, blood-soaked figure. Taking their cue from the King, the druids threw back their heads, and when the laughter died down they resumed their wild dancing. More long minutes passed and Bridey thought she would faint from the heat and the spinning. The music was deafening and now to add to the din came faint rumbles of thunder. Wind gusted through the camp making the flames leap higher. Breagh stepped forward and called for silence, and when the music stopped he spoke to his army in a loud voice.

"The moment is here!" he cried. "The time of Death! It is Samain, the beginning of the New Year, when the Dead come forth in their glory. Bring me the offering! Bring me the poet! We will shed sacred blood and ensure victory on the morrow!"

As the druids clustered round Canola and pulled her to her feet, Bridey made sure that she was among them, close to her friend. Breagh was facing the crowd, his arms outstretched, and the growling thunder grew louder. Beside the King the tall druid stood, golden sickle in hand.

Lightning lit the sky. For an instant everything was clear, every outline stark: the shabby, littered camp; the panting druids; the sick, drunken men. The foot-soldiers saw themselves, grey and tired. They saw the bejewelled warriors near the Tomb, lit for a fraction of a second by the blue light: puppets, jerky and graceless, no longer fearsome. The gaping mouth of the Tomb was an ugly hole, the landscape bleak and sterile. The King stood, sword drawn, beside Canola, and in the lightning flash he was no longer awesome. In the shadow of Brugh na Ngetal, the King was fragile and foolish.

Then came a thunderclap so loud that every man in the camp ducked and covered his ears. Lightning forked to earth on either side of the Tomb, and a row of spindly willows in the marshes became trees of flame whipped by the wind. King Breagh flinched and shielded his eyes. The druids were backing away, their robes billowing, their wild beards blown. The fires sent spiralling columns of sparks into the sky, and in the centre of the camp the King's hut, unable to stand the force of the wind, subsided with a groan of wicker. As the druids fled the Tomb, a golden sickle skittered across the stone and lay harmlessly in shadow.

"Cowards!" screamed the King. "Do you dare disobey . . ." and he whirled round to see the Captain of the Guard slipping away, followed by his men. "Come back! Do you fear thunder more than your King? See what magic I have at my disposal!" But as more thunder split his ear drums, he felt madness swirl around him. Seeing Canola cowering nearby, he smiled desperately. Beside her skulked the last druid. With a hand so sweaty he could barely grasp the pommel of the sword, Breagh raised his heavy blade.

"Stop!"

Prince Lir stood before him, his cloak thrown back, the rings on his fingers catching the light of the fires. He no longer looked like a fawning puppy or a sulky child, and Breagh noticed for the first time the tic that twitched the young man's eye. In front of him Lir held the sickle discarded by the druids. More lightning ripped the sky and Breagh spat contemptuously at his upstart favourite.

"You'll pay dearly for this, you smooth-faced maw-worm!" and slashing down with his blade, he focused on Canola and ran forward.

Eadha, who had been following the Prince like a shadow, stuck out a leg and tripped the King, and Breagh sprawled on the cold stones.

More thunder crashed overhead. Down in the camp, men

cringed and wailed as superstition and exhaustion combined to produce a deadly terror. The captains and druids were desperate to get away from the yawning Tomb, and they tumbled over one another in their haste to escape, their legs snarled in their cloaks. Beneath the noise of the storm could be heard a strange hollow warbling, chords from unseen harps in harmonies unknown to the terrified men. But on the ground lay scattered the pipes and drums of the army: the musicians had fled.

Breagh looked up. Standing together in stolen robes, were Bridey and Canola, framed by the jagged mouth of the Tomb. The King quailed. It was as if a mirror had been split and the two parts set side by side: the same sloping nose and pointed chin, green eyes . . . as alike as two facets of a crystal. Canola's hair flashed silver and her eyes stared unblinking at the fallen King. Breagh gazed at Bridey: white robes stained vivid red, hair black and wild about her face and a crown upon her head, gleaming bright. The face beneath the crown was cool and austere and Breagh swallowed in fear. The Samain fires crackled and still the thunder rumbled. Down below, the men in the camp looked up at the Tomb and began to scream.

Shadowy figures were coming from the open door of Brugh na Ngetal, walking slowly, unperturbed, into the white-blue glare of the lightning. Panic increased at the sight of the strange, slow figures; warriors fled, colliding with the druids, clawing frantically. But wherever they turned they saw the ghostly people: men and women walking slowly through the terrified crowd, whispering and tugging at the clothes of the fleeing men. They seemed solid, fleshy, with their glinting bronze ear-rings, their pale hair and blue tattoos. *We have come back*, they whispered. *We have come back from our hillside to sing you songs and make you happy . . . Oh, we'll sing you such songs . . .*

Men ran this way and that, and all about the lightning flickered. Bronze-clad ghosts laughed, parting red lips to show white teeth. The soldiers wailed, feeling strong fingers plucking at their beards. The storm still raged and the Tuatha dé

Danaan laughed and shook their pale hair and began to chase the sobbing remnants of Breagh's army. On the edge of the camp, the horses reared up and broke their tethers, galloping off, patted on the rump by the playful dead.

Freakish gusts of wind tore the fragile huts from the ground and tossed them into the air where they spiralled round the heads of the soldiers, before crashing to the ground broken and useless. Mad music filled the air, mingling with the thunder and the screams. Bushes thrashed and reeds were flattened, and the ghosts of the Tuatha played among the wreckage of the army camp, inspiring terror with their bronze swords and outlandish laughter.

Bridey and Canola watched but were not afraid. Here were the people from songs and stories, the people from out of their own imaginations – strong and beautiful, with swirling blue on their skin and wild, rippling hair. The Tuatha were savage and wild, but Bridey and Canola were safe: whatever was happening they were part of it.

Lir and Eadha lay near each other on the ground. Eadha was open-mouthed as he watched the dances of the dead, and he held tight to Lir's hand. Lir too was spellbound, certain that this was a dream . . . and yet when a spirit brushed past he felt a cool breeze on his face and the being turned and grinned, eyes bright among whirling tattoos.

Breagh staggered to his feet and watched his men as they ran from the ghosts of long dead kings. His army was gone, broken, and the flags of Connacht sagged and fell among the debris.

"I am the King," he protested. "I, Breagh of the New Hand. I was anointed. I am your ruler. I have the power to . . . who dares disrupt my kingdom? I'll have . . . I'll . . ." But cold fingers plucked at the thick golden band of his crown and someone laughed. His crown fell to the ground and rolled away.

A ghost approached, a tall woman with wild hair and green eyes, who challenged Breagh and made him quake until he felt that his mind was not his own. The woman wore a battle tunic that left her arms bare and across one tattooed shoulder hung a heavy harp. The hem of her tunic was stained, as if dipped in blood, and her cloak was dark and sombre. She stood before Breagh, dwarfing him, and although her words were in a language too old to remember, Breagh understood.

"Your little time of domination is past, King, and your men have fled. You are a frail reed without them, are you not? What power do you have, now your liegemen have gone? Show me, King!" And she laughed. She was savage and ageless – wild hair, eyes the colour of the palest grass, sloping nose and strong pointed chin, broad shoulders shaking and teeth sharp – as she threw back her head and ridiculed the King. Breagh cowered, incapable of striking out. He felt as if he was consumed by ice. He fell to his knees, abject, no longer a king, only a stupefied, frightened man.

The Goddess Brigit watched him crawl away, then turned to Bridey and Canola and for an inexpressable moment the girls met her gaze. Again she spoke in the old guttural language and her eyes sparked.

"Well met, my helpers. My poet and my basket-weaver, greetings."

Bridey licked dry lips and watched Brigit: golden harp, coarsely woven cloak, the long heavy sword slung carelessly from one hip.

"You have triumphed, my friends," she continued. "You have righted the balance. It has called for great courage . . . and great love. The mirror was in danger of shattering but you were valiant. I thank you." She came forward and the girls watched awestruck as she put out a powerful arm. Her hand was strong, with blue arrowheads on every knuckle, and Bridey felt a cool touch on her brow. At the same moment, Canola felt her headache disappear and the tension drain from her neck and shoulders. She felt light, almost weightless.

Bridget gave them one last look, then turned away. Soon she was among the reeds which swayed and shivered as she passed, and the girls saw her disappear among the Tuatha dé Danaan and the last fleeing soldiers.

The entrance was deserted, only Breagh remained. He was transfixed. What powers had been let loose? He had thought he could control the spirits, but these beings were beyond control. He stood motionless, like a rabbit in lantern light. Together, Bridey and Canola turned to face him.

"Go!" they commanded. "Begone!"

Instantly Breagh fled, stumbling into the darkness as the Samain fires dwindled and dimmed and the screams of the soldiers became fainter. The Tuatha dé Danaan were leaving, disappearing behind boulders, vanishing into the trunks of trees, melting away . . .

Bridey and Canola were all at once so tired they could hardly stand. They struggled to get out of their robes, leaning against each other. Bridey put her hand to her head. There was nothing there.

"The crown's gone," she said.

Canola nodded. It began to rain.

Eadha ran up.

"Did you see them?" he shouted. "I wasn't scared!" he tugged at Bridey. "We were captured. This is Lir!"

Bridey grabbed her brother, feeling his thin arms and the fragile curve of his spine. For a fleeting moment she remembered the visions of Eadha trampled by war-lords, remembered the blood-lust and the screams of the dying . . . then it all became elusive, the picture vanished leaving her mind peaceful. Rain streamed down her face.

Canola and Lir stared at each other, a dim recollection growing of an elder brother sent away, leaving a lonely, pale-haired sister. They stood looking at the ground, overcome by confusion. Below, in the wrecked camp, a remaining flag of Connacht flapped feebly in the air, while all over the dark plain the last of Breagh's army sought shelter behind bushes and tumbledown walls.

It was all over.

Nothing could be heard but the sound of the rain and the gentle rattling of the reeds.

epilogue

Six months later, Bridey was in the coracle in the shade of the willow grove. Sunlight pierced the leaves and turned the water amber, and the coracle drifted slowly as Bridey held her dripping paddle still, watching the shady bank and the dazzling lake. Today was Beltine, in the month of Saille the Willow. Tonight the cattle would be driven between the fires and the people would dance sunwise, in circles plotted by Tahan and the Abbess. Bridey would go, to dance and eat Beltine cake.

She sighed and drifted. It was a new coracle, bigger and stronger than the old one which was now properly Eadha's. She had built it during the long winter days, while the lake was frozen and geese sat on the ice all day, sliding about and tapping with their beaks.

She had been glad to get home, and delighted to spend her days weaving baskets and working on the new coracle. Her hands had become stronger and her mother noticed the new work and praised her, "Bridey, this weaving will sell all over Connacht: you will make my fortune yet!"

Bridey sighed, remembering her return to the settlement, the desperate relief of her mother and Sorcha, and their endless angry questions. She and Canola had kept silent about most of what had happened. They discussed it only with each other, in the dim light of the cowshed, while Bridey taught Canola the rudiments of weaving and the poet struggled to get the willow into shape. Eadha, of course, told everyone everything – all about Brigit, the Tuatha dé Danaan and the downfall of Breagh. His friends listened agape at first, until the bragging became incessant, then they pushed him in a puddle and ran off shrieking. Adults listened indulgently, patting him on the head and telling each other that this was what came of letting children run wild.

It had taken them a week to get back from the Tomb, Bridey and Canola riding Ceibhfhionn, Eadha and Lir following on the black pony. They were hungry and dirty and were greeted not triumphantly, but with cuffs and recriminations. What were they, after all, but foolish runaway children, who had worried their mother almost to death? When they told the people that the war was over, they were laughed at and given yarrow and angelica for their colds – they all had coughs and running noses and Bridey herself was feverish and sweating. Her mother put her to bed for a week, allowing herself to pamper her daughter night and day, so grateful was she to see her alive.

Only Abbess Fionnuala and Tahan the Greek seemed to understand their story, and when Bridey was allowed out of bed, the Abbess invited her to the sanctuary where she made her drink catnip and let her doze in front of the fire, waiting for Bridey to speak of her own accord. At last Bridey told her everything – from the day she first saw the crown, to the night she stood by the Tomb and watched the Tuatha dé Danaan rout the King's army. Fionnuala had nodded, poured more catnip, and smiled wistfully as Bridey spoke of Brigit and the touch of cool fingers on her forehead. The candlelight deepened the colours of the tapestries and in the distance Bridey heard the chanting of the convent women at their meditations.

"And what shall you do now, Bridey?" the Abbess had asked finally, lighting a new candle.

Bridey, peaceful and full of catnip, gazed sleepily round the low room and sighed. What more could she want? She looked at the inkhorn and the scrolls of parchment on the table, the thick volumes with their embossed leather covers, decorated with knots and spirals; she remembered Canola's pale head bent over a book . . .

"I shall learn to read," she mused.

"Very well," said Fionnuala. "I shall enjoy teaching you. We can start tomorrow. Now, home to bed with you."

So every afternoon, when work was finished, Bridey walked through the woods to the convent to study the dots and squiggles that slowly became words. Drifting beneath the willows, she rolled them on her tongue, "I am the roaring winter sea, I am the wave that returns to the shore ..." Sometimes Cormac went with her. He found it hard to concentrate, and his bitterness and unhappiness was like a cloud, spoiling her pleasure. But still she took him with her, hoping the lovely words and patterns could help lift the misery that the war had left him with.

The settlement was very different to the way it had been a year ago. The war had left scars, and the harsh winter had taken more lives: it had been a difficult time as the neglected harvest was followed by months of ice and hunger. The surviving men were angry and found no pleasure in life; they were tormented by memories of the war. Bridey hated the changes and responded with anger of her own, escaping to the woods as she had done in the summer.

Canola stayed until the daffodils were out, for the roads were still dangerous with mercenaries. It had been good having her here. They had talked, argued, played, talked more ... Bridey missed her. She felt the familiar twinge of jealousy. Canola had gone back to Corkaguiney with Lir; from there they were to travel further north to visit their parents, "Though they will be most disappointed we didn't fall into a bog and drown," Canola had noted sourly, chewing her fingernails.

It had been unnerving for Canola to find a brother after all the years of longing for one. She and Lir had memories in common that gave her life a new depth. Bridey had been jealous, but had held her tongue. Lir was not a prince any more, just an ordinary boy, helping Bres the swineherd. Now he smelled of pigs instead of perfume.

For Bridey herself there was only one place she belonged, and that was here, in the cluster of huts on the marshy shores of the lake. She wondered if she would ever be able to leave her family, leave her work? Dipping her paddle in the water, she watched the ripples widen...

Later, when she knew more, when she had discovered all that was in the books at the convent... She sighed again deeply and began to paddle slowly home. Far out, the current flowed south.